ling

KT-381-390

LOVE TRIUMPHANT

Steve Baxter disappears while interior designer Lizzie Hilton is working on the refurbishment of his property. His brother, Todd, suspects Lizzie of becoming romantically involved with Steve, knowing that he is due to come into an inheritance upon marriage. Lizzie challenges Todd to find evidence to substantiate his outrageous allegation. But when Paul Owen appears on the scene Lizzie panics — because Paul can provide Todd with the evidence he is looking for . . .

MARGARET MOUNSDON

LOVE TRIUMPHANT

Complete and Unabridged

LINFORD
Leicester

First published in Great Britain in 2012

First Linford Edition
published 2013

A catalogue record for this book is available
from the British Library.

ISBN 978–1–4448–1541–2

Published by
F. A. Thorpe (Publishing)
Anstey, Leicestershire

Set by Words & Graphics Ltd.
Anstey, Leicestershire
Printed and bound in Great Britain by
T. J. International Ltd., Padstow, Cornwall

This book is printed on acid-free paper

Striking A Deal

'I simply can't believe it. I would never have known. It's remarkable.'

'I can assure you it's true.' Olivia's throaty chuckle dissolved into a hacking cough. 'It really is me.'

Lizzie Hilton watched in concern as the older woman groped for a tissue.

'Sorry, darling.' Olivia dabbed delicately at her eyes that were still streaming with amusement. 'Too many years spent in smoky dance halls.'

While she gulped down some water Lizzie returned her attention to the framed photo of the girl on the piano. She was young, doe-eyed, fresh-faced and dressed as a flapper in a fringed black dress, long black gloves that reached above her elbows and a sparkly bandeau wound around her chestnut brown hair. She also sported a huge pink feather adornment over her left ear. The splash of colour created a startling contrast to the rest of her outfit.

'I had the men running after me, I can tell you,' Olivia, who had now regained her breath, informed Lizzie. 'Stage door Johnnies we used to call them. They would turn up after the show and offer us all sorts of outrageous gifts, from flowers to champagne. I returned them, of course. You never knew where that sort of thing might lead but I have to admit I let them take me out to dinner if I was hungry, which I usually was in those days. I was escorted to the best places in town and wined and dined like royalty.' Olivia's wicked smile lit up her face. 'Of course once I met my darling Monty all that changed.'

'Is this Monty?'

Lizzie held up another photograph of a rather dashing young man standing nonchalantly in front of an early touring car, his foot on the dashboard. He was wearing a tweed suit and sporting a colourful Fair Isle jumper.

'Yes.' Olivia's eyes softened. 'They say love has no rules, don't they?'

Lizzie had to acknowledge this was true.

'I mean, there was I, not to put too fine a point on it, living a slightly racy life, racketing about all over the place with a string of sweethearts, while Monty was the epitome of respectability.'

'How did the two of you meet?' Lizzie asked.

'We were introduced by a friend of his. He'd dragged Monty along to a matinee. As Monty had a car, his friend inveigled him to come along and cadged a lift off him. The friend was your typical stage door Johnny and he talked his way into the dressing-rooms afterwards. Poor Monty looked so uncomfortable with all the frills and fripperies draped about the place, but from the moment I first saw him I was smitten. He was so effortlessly handsome, a real gentleman. It took ages to get him to fall in love with me.'

'Surely not.' Lizzie put the photograph back on the coffee table.

'Darling, you do not know the half of it. I pulled out all the stops, but his mother didn't approve of me and put every obstacle she could in the way of our romance. I can't say I blame her. I must have been a bit of a shock. She invited me to afternoon tea and I committed the cardinal sin of breaking a cup.' Olivia started laughing again at the memory.

Lizzie laughed with her. Outrageous though she was, she couldn't help liking Olivia Baxter. She was so full of life.

'I tried the tweed skirt, cashmere jumper, row of pearls bit, but it didn't seem right. Eventually I wore whatever I fancied and that was when Monty finally fell in love with me. He said it was because I wasn't pretending any more to be someone I wasn't. Can you believe it? He actually liked my outrageous outfits?'

'But his mother didn't?'

Olivia shook her head. 'She wasn't a bad old stick really and after Roger was born she thawed and we began to rub along. She absolutely doted on her grandson and for that alone my feelings towards her changed, but we weren't really on the same wavelength. My father was a railway worker and my mother served in a shop and,' the impish twinkle was back in Olivia's eyes, 'I was born in Clapham, south of the river.'

'What's wrong with that?' Lizzie demanded.

'Absolutely nothing, darling, but my mother-in-law was a crashing snob and she had higher ideas for her beloved only son. When she learned I was a dancer and on the stage she nearly expired on the spot.' Olivia began coughing with laughter again. 'If it hadn't been for George, my father-in-law, I don't think I would have stood a chance with Monty.'

Two large over-excited dogs raced into the room and began running around in circles, their tails narrowly missing several fine china ornaments.

'Get down for goodness' sake,' Olivia ordered them. 'You can have a walk later when I've finished talking to Miss Hilton. Where was I?'

Lizzie sneaked a look at her watch. Much as she was enjoying his grandmother's company, she'd been here over an hour and there was no sign of Steve.

'Your father-in-law?' Lizzie replied.

'That's right. George was a lovely man. Luckily he liked me so as his word was law in the Baxter household, I was in. Monty was their only child and I think George always wanted a daughter.' Her face crinkled into amusement again. 'So there you have it, a potted history of my life. Monty and I had our ups and downs, but this house has always been a family home despite my mother-in-law's interference.' Olivia sniggered. 'Do you know she once tried to scare the wits out of me by telling me the place was haunted?'

'Is it?' Lizzie asked.

'No idea. Ma in law spun me some tale about an errant knight who came here to woo his ladylove then was banished to France for his troubles. So the story goes the silly man came back and was caught in her arms. The girl was exiled to a convent. I don't know what happened to him but every so often he's supposed to a spot of haunting.' A smile of reminiscence crossed Olivia's face.

'Have I offered you any tea?' Olivia glanced at the giant watch on her left wrist.

'No, thank you.' Lizzie blinked, trying to catch up with the speed of Olivia's change of subject. 'I really only dropped by to see Steve.'

'What do you want with my grandson?' Olivia asked.

Lizzie hesitated. 'He hasn't told you?'

'No he hasn't, but I won't put you on the spot by insisting on an answer. It's absolutely none of my business what he gets up to, but a word of warning in your ear. He likes to play the field. I think he's inherited my genes.' Olivia looked Lizzie up and down. 'I must say, though, I wouldn't have thought you were his type. You look far too independent to me. He goes for the clingy types.' Olivia shuddered.

'I'm not actually a girlfriend.' Lizzie began wondering how much of her relationship with Steve she should disclose.

'Good to hear it. You and I, we're feisty, wouldn't you say?'

Although they had only just met, Lizzie had to admit Olivia's character analysis was spot on. Lizzie's independence of spirit had been her downfall on more than one occasion.

'You do have another grandson, don't you?'

'Todd?' Olivia made a face. 'You know I love both my grandsons equally, but Todd can at times be a little like my late lamented mother-in-law.'

'You mean he's a snob?'

'Not at all. He's,' Olivia hesitated,

'how can I put it? He's not exactly the easiest person in the world to deal with.'

'He doesn't suffer fools gladly?'

'To be fair he's got a good business head on his shoulders and I've no fault with the way he manages the day to day running of the industrial unit. We all agreed Steve would be no good at that sort of thing. He is the artist in the family. He designs houses and in his spare time does beautiful ornamental turning. Have you seen his woodwork?'

Lizzie shook her head.

'You must get him to show you some time. It's creative stuff, so imaginative. It quite takes my breath away. He's won prizes you know.'

'I'll look forward to seeing his work. I also look forward to meeting Todd,' Lizzie felt obliged to add, although from what Olivia had told her, she doubted they would see eye to eye.

Olivia leaned forward, a confidential look on her face. 'Another word in your ear.'

There was something about the expression on Olivia's face that warned Lizzie she might not like what she was about to hear.

'Don't let him browbeat you.'

'Steve?'

'I'm talking about Todd.'

'Why should Todd browbeat me?'

'I, well, I know I shouldn't interfere. Todd runs the show and all that, but I like to have people I bond with occupying the industrial units.'

'Olivia, what have you done?' Lizzie's suspicions were now fully aroused.

'Nothing,' she replied, widening her eyes and, for a moment, Lizzie caught a glimpse of the playful girl she had once been.

Olivia sighed. 'I always was dreadful at telling fibs,' she muttered.

'I don't want either of us getting into trouble with your grandson. Olivia, look at me, please.'

The older woman raised a reluctant pair of brown eyes. 'You're going to lecture me, aren't you?'

'Have you quoted me a low rate for my unit tenancy?'

'I can charge what I like.' Olivia now picked at the fringed edge of the chenille cloth covering a side table.

'I think you'll find you can't, Olivia. These things are laid down in the lease.'

'I'm a partner in the business. It's all in black and white somewhere and you're not to bully me.' She thrust out her lower lip in a gesture of defiance.

'I'm not bullying you, but a business must be run along viable lines,' Lizzie pointed out, 'otherwise it runs into problems.'

'Let's not talk about it now.' Olivia waved a beringed hand at Lizzie. 'You're young and beautiful, and I've always loved people with auburn hair. I am in a position to offer you some help so let's hear no more about business viability. I never understand that sort of thing anyway and don't worry about Todd. I'll fix things up with him.'

Lizzie bit her lip. There was no doubt Olivia's offer would provide a more than welcome boost to her business plan. Market forces had vastly exceeded Lizzie's initial costings.

'Good, that's all settled then.' Olivia took her silence for assent. 'Now, do you want me to pass on a message to Steve? It looks as though he might have been held up.'

Lizzie bit down her annoyance. The customer was always king but there were limits. This wasn't the first time he had let her down.

'Irritating I know, darling, but Steve keeps his own hours. Now, sorry to hurry you along,' Olivia urged, 'but it's my bridge evening.'

'Would you ask Steve to contact me when convenient?' Lizzie took the hint.

'Leave it with me,' Olivia promised, 'and don't worry about the other business. I'll fix things with Todd.'

On the drive back to her flat in the neighbouring village of Maiden Magna, Lizzie couldn't help thinking about the Baxter family. Montague Baxter had in the past been a significant presence in

Maiden Poultry, the larger of the two villages. His grandfather had been the local Justice of the Peace and the family could trace its ancestry way back to the Doomsday Book. The Baxters had lived in Maiden Farm, a classic Dorset farmhouse for generations.

It was situated on the edge of the village and no longer a working farm. Over the years much of the land had been sold off to raise capital to meet death duties and tax demands.

When Steve Baxter had contacted Lizzie and requested she provide estimates for the refurbishment of the cottage he was purchasing she could not believe her luck. He had been one of her first proper commissions and she was determined to make a success of it.

'May I ask how you found out about me?' Lizzie asked, when they met up for coffee in The Copper Kettle to discuss details.

'I saw your advert in the newsagents,' he said. 'Mrs Godwin, the lady who runs the shop, gave you a glowing reference.'

'Good old Mrs Godwin.' Lizzie smiled.

A small dimple tugged at the corner of Steve's mouth, softening his expression. 'May I suggest you lighten up and tuck into a cream cake? I'm going to have one and the bill is on me, no expense spared. What about that pink squashy thing? I fancy the gooey chocolate one.' Steve nudged the cake stand towards her. 'I hope you're not on a diet.'

'I don't have time.'

'Good.' Steve lobbed the pink cake on to her plate. 'Where are your premises, by the way?'

Lizzie forked up some of her pink sponge cake. 'That's a bit of a sore question.'

'Is there a problem?' Steve queried.

'I've been looking for an affordable unit for ages,' Lizzie confessed. 'But everywhere is so pricey.'

'A lot of incomers have upped

property prices. It's a source of local discontent.'

'If I do find somewhere within my budget it's either damp or situated in a not very nice area.'

'Then I could be the answer to your dream.' Steve beamed at her.

'You could?'

'Baxter's Industrial Park. Have you heard of it?'

A large lump of pink icing plopped back on to Lizzie's plate.

'You're that Baxter?'

'One of them.'

'Thanks for trying to help, but I could never afford your rates.'

'Never is a word we do not use.' Steve dismissed her objection with a wave of his hand. 'Leave it to me I'll speak to my grandmother. She'll fix you up.'

Lizzie knew she should have guessed the pair of them had cooked something up between them. In order to release more capital after a downturn in the money market, Montague Baxter had decided to convert a patch of land into business use and a dozen or so select units had been erected on what had originally been open farmland. No expense had been spared. The approach road was a proper paved driveway with a private dedicated entrance and each unit was stand-alone and all had marvellous views of the coastal scenery. A twenty-four-hour security surveillance system was in operation and every night the unit was secured by huge barred gates ensuring absolute safety on site. The rental reflected this state of the art service and Lizzie hadn't even bothered to read the glossy brochure that had plopped through her letter-box, advertising their facilities.

Todd and his brother, Steve, had inherited control of the units and now ran it jointly with their grandmother, Olivia, Todd being the senior partner and the member of the family responsible for most of the business decisions.

'Come up and have a look round,'

Steve urged her, 'Before we come to any decision.'

Lizzie had loved the unit Steve suggested she should occupy from the moment he had showed it to her.

'What about bank references?' Lizzie ran a finger over a workbench that had been placed in a far corner. It was smooth and she loved the smell of fresh pinewood.

'Our financial people will get in touch with you, but don't worry, there won't be a problem,' had been Steve's reply. 'Do you like the workbench?' he asked, noting her interest.

'Very much.'

'I made it,' Steve said with a shy smile. 'I've done all the wood finishing. It's a hobby of mine.'

At the end of the week Lizzie received an official contract in the post, which she had immediately studied in detail, then signed and returned. Two days later a courier delivered a set of shiny new keys.

'I thought you lived at Maiden

Farm.' Lizzie finished her cake with a contented sigh.

'I do.'

'Then why on earth do you want to leave it?'

Lizzie had occasionally glimpsed the farmhouse through the trees when she had driven past. With its paddocks and landscaped gardens it looked a beautiful place to live.

'The thing is, I love my grandmother dearly, but living with a grandparent at the age of twenty-six does rather cramp a young man's style.'

'Surely there's enough room at Maiden Farm for you to have your independence?'

'My grandmother has to be the nosiest person in the world. She doesn't sleep that well and often roams about the house making cups of tea and watching late-night television shows to pass the time. She has this habit of drifting into my part of the house in search of company. When Olivia sees I've got a visitor, well, she sort of stays.

No amount of hinting can budge her off the sofa.'

'You have my deepest sympathy,' Lizzie commiserated with him.

'I wouldn't mind but I've met someone I think is really special and until I'm sure she feels the same way about me, I want to keep her away from the family. So do you think you could be a sport and keep quiet about our little business arrangement?'

'Of course,' Lizzie agreed, glad the favour had turned out to be a relatively mild one. 'Your grandmother won't hear of your plans from me.'

* * *

Lizzie parked her car at the back of the newsagents in the slot Mrs Godwin always kept free for her.

'Yoo hoo,' Charlotte, her granddaughter, waved vigorously out of the back door.

Today she was wearing denim shorts over black and white striped tights and an orange T-shirt. In her hair she sported a colourful array of combs and ribbons.

Lizzie waved back. Despite her challenging dress sense she liked Charlotte. She was a vibrant youngster and she and her younger brother often slept over with their grandmother.

'We're doing one of our special curries tonight. You have to join us. My best friend, Nadia, and I need help with our French conversation.'

'I'll be there,' Lizzie promised.

'Cool. See you at eight. *Au revoir.*' Charlotte blew her a kiss before disappearing back inside the shop.

Lizzie mounted the steps to the little flat she occupied over the shop. There was just about time to map out a few ideas and have a shower before her curry supper.

Interfering Siblings

Lizzie loved living in the West Country village of Maiden Magna. No-one quite knew the origin of the name. Lizzie had looked it up, but all she could discover was that the neighbouring Maiden Poultry had something to do with chicken rustling in the late seventeenth century. The details were as sketchy as the origins of the names of the two villages.

Whatever, being close to the sea was another bonus and she spent much of her precious free time down in the cove, watching the sailing enthusiasts tack to and fro on the water.

Marram grass and dunes backed on to the sheltered sandy beach and when she could Lizzie spent lazy weekend afternoons enjoying an egg sandwich picnic and watching the world go by. Occasionally when finances allowed she finished the afternoon off by treating herself to some fresh crab. The local fishermen were pleased to sell their catch off cheaply to their regulars and Jem, her favourite fisherman, often kept one back for her.

'It's a beauty and no mistake,' he would say as he prepared the shell for her. 'Special occasion, is it?'

'Not really.' Lizzie always shied off answering personal questions.

Her past was still too raw in her memory to indulge freely in casual conversation. Being a man of the sea, Jem understood and didn't pry, but several of the die-hard locals regarded Lizzie with suspicion. She had moved into the area six months earlier and had done very little to mix socially with the residents. The usual leaflets had been thrust through her letter-box, inviting her to newcomer welcome evenings, coffee mornings and bring and buy sales, but Lizzie declined them all.

Mrs Godwin was the only neighbour who had not taken no for an answer and forced Lizzie into accepting her invitations to supper.

'I won't ask questions,' she insisted, 'but everyone needs company. You can meet my granddaughter, Charlotte and her brother, Alan. They are lovely youngsters and I don't like to think of you on your own up in the flat.'

She stood up, brushing grass off her jeans. For the first time in months she was looking forward to the coming week. Steve had definitive ideas on the decor of his cottage and Lizzie had promised to drop by his new premises later in the evening to discuss options with him. She had received a hurried late night telephone call from him after several more of the dates he had made to meet up had been broken.

'Sorry,' he whispered down the telephone, 'Olivia's on the prowl. I can't talk any louder. The phone's in the corridor and I'm sure she suspects I'm up to something.'

'Haven't you got a mobile?' Lizzie found she was whispering back at him.

'Forgot to charge it and it's been a beast of a day. I've been in meeting after meeting so I couldn't call you from work. Never take up the profession of an architect.'

'I won't,' Lizzie promised solemnly.

'And never accept a commission from a health club. It's all green issues and what can you do on a shoestring? If I'm bald next time you see me, you'll know why. I'm tearing my hair out in handfuls.'

'Poor you,' Lizzie sympathised. 'Are you sure you want to go through with this commission?'

After so many broken dates Lizzie was beginning to suspect he was telephoning to say it was all off.

'A Baxter's word is his bond. Look out.'

'What?' Lizzie ducked then, feeling foolish, straightened up. She heard a muffled exchange down the end of the line.

'Sorry. Olivia wanted to know who was on the other end of the line. Look, do you think you could pop round the day after tomorrow in the evening say?'

'To Maiden Farm?'

'No.' Steve raised his voice in alarm. 'We can't meet here,' he added in a quieter voice.

'Where then?'

'Have you heard of Wrenn Close?'

'If you give me the postcode I'll find it.'

'By the way I'm sure you won't bump into him, but if you do, you won't mention it will you?' Steve said.

Lizzie, who had been scribbling a few notes on the pad she always kept handy, blinked down the telephone receiver. 'Who?' she asked, perplexed.

'My brother, Todd.'

'What about him?'

'He's due back home soon.'

'And where would I be bumping into him?'

'Todd has a nasty habit of finding out what's going on in my life.'

'I haven't told a soul.'

'I wasn't suggesting you had, but I

wouldn't put it past Todd to get wind of my plans. He's quite capable of tracking me down and hanging around outside Wrenn Close if only to see what's happening.'

The more Lizzie heard of Steve's older brother, the more she didn't like him. He sounded too much like Paul Owen for comfort.

'Surely your private life is none of your brother's business?'

'Try telling that to Todd. He's only two years older than me but ever since we lost our parents when we were children and moved in with Olivia and Monty, he's looked out for me. I'm grateful and all that, but now I'm at an age when I'm more than capable of looking after myself.'

'Have you tried telling Todd?'

'I don't want to hurt his feelings.'

'Ask him how he would like it. I'm sure that would make him see your point of view.'

'Perhaps I will when I haven't got quite so much on my plate. Anyway, if

I'm delayed getting to our appointment, or anything like that, I'll leave you a note. There's a key under the mat. Let yourself in.'

Back at her flat Lizzie decided there should be time for a quick look through her notes and ideas before she set out for Wrenn Close.

To her relief there were no messages on her answer phone and Mrs Godwin hadn't reported any visitors. Lizzie still couldn't shake off the feeling that Paul Owen might discover her whereabouts and come looking for her. She had learned to her cost he was a man who did not like to be crossed.

To be doubly certain where she was going, Lizzie glanced briefly at a map of the area before she set out. Steve had told her Wrenn Close was situated in a small village, Coombe St Giles, about ten miles from Maiden Magna.

Although it was little more than a hamlet, Lizzie found it with ease and as she drove along the winding main street she was surprised to discover Wrenn

Close was not a new executive development as she had imagined, but a row of period cottages, terraced and facing on to a village green that bore evidence of a cricket pitch.

Lizzie parked her car in the road outside. Although it was only half-past nine at night there was no-one about and the atmosphere was eerily still. She wouldn't have thought Wrenn Close was the type of place to appeal to Steve, but perhaps it was solitude he was looking for, a sentiment Lizzie knew all about.

An owl hooted as she opened her driver's door. Coombe St Giles appeared to comprise a Norman church, an inn that was shuttered, a cricket club, also locked up and a shop. Lizzie caught shadowed movement behind the glass windows. She hesitated, wondering if she ought to ask if she was in the right place, when the decision was taken out of her hands. The shop door was shut in one firm movement and the *Open* sign turned round to read *Closed*.

'So much for friendly locals,' Lizzie murmured to herself.

Lizzie hoisted her sample satchel on to her shoulder then, picking up her tote bag, headed towards number six and knocked on the door. There was no reply, but the key was under the mat exactly where Steve said it would be and to Lizzie's relief she felt it turn smoothly in the lock.

'Hello?' she called out. 'Anybody home?'

The rooms were in darkness. Reluctant to switch on the lights, Lizzie put down her bags and scooped up some junk mail that was lying on the mat. Steve hadn't given her his mobile number and stupidly she hadn't thought to ask him for it. There was no way of checking if he would be further delayed and whether or not it would be worth her while waiting.

Lizzie flicked a switch and the hall was immediately bathed in yellow light. She sniffed. Someone had been polishing the staircase with beeswax. It was a comforting smell and reminded her of her childhood. She crossed to a small door and opened it. Although the room was unfurnished and her footsteps echoed on the bare flooring, Lizzie could see it would make a comfortable lounge.

A property such as this was special and would need careful attention. The swatches she had brought with her would not be suitable. This was the sort of cottage that called out for traditional furnishings not the contemporary style statement she had imagined Steve would want.

To Lizzie's delight she discovered a small garden at the back. It was overgrown but nothing a little tender loving care couldn't put right. She pushed open a French window and imagined a vegetable plot with rows of runner beans growing up the side fence and perhaps a flower-bed of bright petunias, something colourful to mark out the middle of the lawn. She took a deep breath of night air.

She closed the door and turned back into the lounge. The church bell chimed ten o'clock. As usual Steve was late. Lizzie began to feel a twinge of unease prickle up the back of her spine. She was alone in a cottage that wasn't hers. It was late at night and, being in the heart of the country, extremely dark. There was no way Paul Owen could track her down here.

After half an hour's fruitless waiting around, Lizzie placed the pile of mail on the window-sill and decided not to wait any longer. Steve would be tired after his long day and in no mood to discuss décor. For her purposes she had absorbed enough of the atmosphere of the cottage to enable her to work on a few suggestions.

Searching round for a pencil she began to scrawl a note on the back of one of Steve's envelopes. Lost in her task she did not notice the door behind her slowly open.

'What the blazes do you think you're

doing?' A crisp voice came at her like a whiplash. Lizzie's pencil fell out of her fingers and rolled across the floor.

Heart thumping she bit down a shriek of shock. Although she knew it was fanciful thinking, a part of her had been expecting Paul Owen to be standing in the doorway.

'Who are you?' she demanded as she looked into a pair of hostile brown eyes.

'I think I asked first,' he replied, the tone of his voice showing no sign of softening.

'That's as may be but I have permission to be here.'

Lizzie stuck out her chin and tossed back her hair, mentally thanking Paul. If it hadn't been for his past treatment of her she would never have known she possessed the courage to stand up to a bully.

The man standing in front of her was tall and dressed in dark shirt and casual dark trousers. He looked as though he hadn't shaved that day and the stubble on his face, coupled with his unfriendly expression, leant him an air of menace.

'Very well,' he acknowledged her words with the briefest of nods. 'My name is Todd Baxter.'

It was all Lizzie could do not to gulp. Why hadn't she guessed his identity?

'You're Steve's brother?' Her voice was not as assured as she would have liked it to be.

'I am and you clearly have the advantage over me. As I still have no idea who you are perhaps you would now do me the honour of introducing yourself.'

'Lizzie Hilton,' she said.

'I presume you are here to meet Steve?'

'Why I am here is none of your business,' Lizzie retaliated.

'It is when you are on my brother's property without his permission.'

'I do have his permission to be here,' Lizzie replied, 'and you'll have to take my word for it,' she added, wishing Steve hadn't sworn her to secrecy.

Todd seemed to be considering her

reply. 'I know the reason for your presence?'

'I'm not falling for that one.'

'I beg your pardon?' One eyebrow was raised in a gesture of interrogation.

'You want to lull me into a false sense of security then get me to babble out all sorts of nonsense. Well,' Lizzie crossed her arms defiantly, 'I'm not going to.'

'Aren't you indeed?' Todd looked as though he wasn't used to being challenged. After the briefest of hesitations, his mouth softened.

'Have I said something to amuse you?' Lizzie demanded.

'I hadn't expected you to be quite so feisty.'

'Since we've only this moment met I fail to see how you could have formed any sort of opinion of me.'

'Now there you are wrong. My grandmother told me all about you.'

'Olivia did? Why?'

'Because she's worried Steve has got involved in another of his foolish schemes.'

'I am not a foolish scheme.'

'I didn't say you were.'

'Steve told me all about you and how you are always poking your nose into his affairs.'

Lizzie bit her lip, reluctant to get into confrontation with Steve's older brother. Whatever personal baggage they shared it was none of her business.

'Look,' she attempted to ease the tension, 'I'm not here to create friction between the pair of you.'

The expression on Todd's face gave nothing away.

'How did you find out about this place anyway?' Lizzie asked intrigued.

'Olivia discovered a scrap of paper in Steve's waste paper bin. It had this address on it.'

'She shouldn't snoop and you shouldn't read your brother's private correspondence.'

'It wasn't a letter. I didn't know what it was. Olivia gave it to me because she thought it might be important.'

'Can't you let your brother lead his own life?'

'Not when there is an inheritance involved.'

'I don't know what you are talking about.'

'Then let me refresh your memory. According to the terms of our parents' bequest, Steve is due to come into his legacy when he gets married. Getting her hands on a sizeable chunk of a very successful industrial estate is quite a temptation for any female, wouldn't you say?'

'And you think that's why I'm here?'

Lizzie was enjoying herself. She hoped she would be around when Todd Baxter found out how wrong he was. He deserved to be taken down a peg or two and as for his suspicions about what she was up to with Steve, her jaw tightened and her eyes flashed with annoyance.

'I don't know what to think but can you understand my concern about who he gets involved with?'

'I am not involved with Steve. Neither am I interested in any inheritance.'

'You did have an appointment to meet him here tonight?'

'Yes, but it's not what you think.'

'It never is and don't bother trying to invent a good story. I've heard them all before.'

'I wouldn't bother wasting my breath. Now if you'll excuse me?'

'Where are you going?'

'That is none of your business.'

'Aren't you going to finish your note to Steve?' Todd stooped down and picked up her pencil. 'You were writing to him I presume?'

'Yes, I was.' Lizzie put out a hand.

'Lizzie Hilton?' Todd frowned.

'Yes?'

'This envelope is addressed to you.'

'What?'

Todd was holding the pile of letters she had placed on the window ledge. As she reached forward to take her envelope out of his grasp Todd held it away from her.

'Not so fast.'

'You've no right to interfere with my correspondence.'

Todd ripped open the envelope. 'Shall we see what my little brother has to say?'

A Dangerous Visitor

Lizzie watched Todd cast his eyes over Steve's letter. Bottling up her emotions was something she thought she had managed to conquer, but Todd's attitude was stretching her self-control to the limit.

Experience had taught her the wisdom of retaining dignity in these sorts of situations, but it wasn't easy with someone as testing as Todd Baxter.

'May I now be permitted to read my own correspondence?' she enquired after a few moments, as Todd skimmed the contents and displayed no intention of handing over the letter.

'*I don't want my grandmother or my brother to know anything about our plans,*' Todd ignored her request and began reading aloud the contents of Steve's letter. '*If I don't manage to make our rendezvous please carry on normally and I will be in touch as soon as I can. It's proving extremely difficult keeping my grandmother in the dark and with Todd due back any moment I think we'll have our work cut out to keep our plans secret. Sorry to involve you in such a cloak and dagger operation but I'm sure things will come right in the end.'*

Lizzie raised her eyes in exasperation. Although she was sure it hadn't been his intention, Steve had made her situation worse. There was no way Todd would believe Lizzie's protestations of innocence now.

'Let me explain,' she began.

'I think Steve's letter says it all. I'm sorry to disappoint you but it looks like he won't be turning up tonight, doesn't it?'

'Yes,' Lizzie agreed.

'Obviously I found out about his plans in time.'

'No, you didn't.' Lizzie flared up. 'You didn't find out about anything.

40

You've got totally the wrong end of the stick.'

'Have I?' Todd didn't look convinced. 'I'm prepared to give you the benefit of the doubt if you would like to tell me exactly what you are doing late at night in Steve's cottage.'

Lizzie hesitated.

'I can't,' she admitted.

'Your powers of invention appear to have deserted you, Miss Hilton.'

'Look, the simplest thing for you to do, instead of throwing wild accusations at me, is to contact your brother. He'll explain everything.'

'I've tried his mobile but my messages keep going to voice mail and he's not at Maiden Farm.' Todd glanced at his watch. 'I've left my grandmother there alone, something I don't like doing at this late hour.'

Lizzie picked up her satchel of samples.

'In that case I won't detain you any longer and if you've nothing further to say to me I'll be on my way.'

41

'I see you came prepared for a quick getaway. I'm sorry you've been disappointed.'

'No, you're not.' Lizzie hefted her other bag on to her shoulder. 'You know your trouble? You're a control freak. You won't always be able to run Steve's life. Getting away from you will be the making of him.'

'So you admit the pair of you did have plans?'

The look of satisfaction on Todd's face was too much for Lizzie. Annoyed with herself for letting that bit of information slip, she moved towards the door. Todd put a hand out as if to detain her.

'There's no need to search my bags. I haven't made off with the teaspoons. As you can see the cottage is empty.'

'I don't know how to get in touch with you.'

'Good,' Lizzie replied. 'Because I have no wish to ever see you again.'

The flicker of uncertainty in Todd's dark brown eyes went a little way towards easing her anger.

'Wait,' he called after her. 'I need your number.'

'No, you don't.' Lizzie turned back towards him. 'Despite your suspicions about my relationship with Steve it has absolutely nothing to do with you. Good night.'

Leaving Todd standing in the middle of the room, Lizzie stalked out of the cottage.

In the road outside she took a deep breath. She could feel Todd's eyes burning a hole in her back.

Throwing her equipment into the back of her rented van, Lizzie yanked open the driver's door. She had so much riding on this commission and now it looked as though it had fallen through.

She should have realised the Baxters of this world operated on a different planet to everyone else. One lost contract wouldn't matter much to them. To Lizzie it was make or break.

She turned the key in the ignition.

The engine turned over then died.

'Don't let me down.' She ground her teeth together and gripped the steering wheel tightly. 'Please,' she begged, 'I promise I'll get you a new battery as soon as I can.'

After a few more coughs the van finally spluttered into life.

'Thank you, thank you,' Lizzie whispered, then not daring to look back at the cottage in case Todd Baxter was on her tail, she pushed her foot down on the accelerator and headed home to Maiden Magna.

Charlotte was patrolling the pavement outside her flat.

'There you are,' she greeted Lizzie with a smile. 'I've been waiting ages for you.'

'Is there a problem?' Lizzie asked.

'You've had a visitor,' Charlotte said, 'a man.'

Lizzie wrestled her satchel out of the back of the van. 'Did he give a name?'

'No.'

'Did he say what he wanted?'

'There was something creepy about him. That's why I was looking out for you, Lizzie. I know it was a fib but I pretended I didn't know you.' Her young face was screwed up in concern. 'Are we still friends?'

'Of course we're still friends and you haven't done anything wrong,' Lizzie assured the young girl. 'Now hadn't you better get back indoors?'

'Gran's out. It's her bingo night. Mum's here. She knows where I am. She would have waited with me but she didn't want to leave Alan alone. He's got the football team staying over. That's why I came outside to get away from the noise. I found this man looking for you. Lizzie. Is he the reason you don't talk to anyone in the village apart from us?'

Lizzie hesitated. It wasn't fair to involve Charlotte in her past. 'What did he look like?' she asked.

'He had this, like, business suit on and funny eyes. He reminded me of the reptiles in Alan's books. I hope he doesn't come back.'

'I shouldn't worry about him.' Lizzie did her best to sound upbeat. From Charlotte's description she was certain Paul Owen was her unwelcome visitor.

The young girl broke into a happy smile, her fears dissolved by Lizzie's reassurance.

'Did you have a good evening? Want any help with your stuff?'

The two girls climbed up the steps to the flat and after Charlotte opened the door they deposited the bags in the hall.

'Thanks, Charlotte.'

'It's Charlie,' she complained. 'Charlotte was my great aunt.'

'Thanks, Charlie,' Lizzie emphasised the name. 'Now off you go, and thanks again.'

'My mum says that's what neighbours are for, to help each other out.' She waved at Lizzie. 'Bye. Sleep well.'

★ ★ ★

The sun pouring through her bedroom window woke her up. Lizzie yawned and stretched. Ahead of her was a day of delivering pamphlets and exercising her charm on shopkeepers in an effort to persuade them to display one of her posters in their windows.

Aware that it had been the simplest of index cards that had caught Steve's attention in Mrs Godwin's window Lizzie also had a ready stock of those to hand, together with an ample supply of cheerful business cards.

She flung open her bedroom window. Things always seemed better in the morning and as she looked down into the street below it held none of the lurking fears of the night before.

The green grocer opposite sweeping his frontage waved up at her. In a spontaneous gesture Lizzie returned his wave. She decided it really was time she made more of an effort to integrate into village life.

She poured out a glass of fresh orange juice and began to go through her paperwork, highlighting potential leads and marking contacts that could prove useful.

Steve Baxter, she decided, was flaky and there was no point pursuing him any further. Secret assignations in country cottages late at night were not recognised business practices of hers and not something she cared to repeat, especially when Todd Baxter was involved in the scenario. She shuddered as she recalled their confrontation then scored through Steve's name.

As she updated her business plan her mobile leapt into life.

'Darling?'

'Mum, where are you?' Lizzie asked.

'At a luxury hotel in the Far East,' came the prompt reply.

'Lucky you,' was Lizzie's envious reply.

'Not as lucky as you would believe. Being personal assistant to a high-powered businessman is not a bed of roses.'

'Convince me.' Lizzie smiled down the line.

'I've hardly been outside the complex since we arrived. It's been a constant stream of meetings, rescheduled appointments and goodness knows how many functions to arrange. I could be anywhere in the world. I dare not look out of the window in case the sight of the blue sky and golden beaches proves too much for me and I do a runner.'

'You know you love your work,' Lizzie chided her mother.

'Yes, I do,' she admitted, 'but right now I would give anything to be on a sunbed sipping a fruit cocktail and watching the world go by. Anyway, how are things with you?'

'Fine.'

'You sure?' Angela Hilton's voice was full of doubt. 'This is your mother you are speaking to.'

'Things are a bit difficult at the moment,' Lizzie admitted. 'A hopeful contract has fallen through, but I've got lots of feelers out.'

'You know there's always a job for you here.'

'Thanks, Mum, I do know that, but I need to make my own way in the world.'

'I don't see why if I'm ready to give a helping hand.'

'You've done enough for me, Mum.'

After the early loss of her husband, Angela had applied for the position of housekeeper to a European diplomat. The job had provided a cottage for her to bring up her daughters and when the diplomat had returned to Belgium, Angela and the children had gone with him.

Angela's natural charm and efficiency had been an asset to the diplomat and she had often acted as his hostess in an official capacity in the absence of his wife. The girls had been educated at an international school in Brussels and during the holidays they had enjoyed travelling round Europe with their mother in a camper van, stopping off wherever the mood took them. It had been an idyllic existence and broadened both girls' social skills and understanding of all cultures.

'I don't wish to sound ungrateful, Mum. I know you're always there if ever I need you, and that's a great consolation, but I have to do my own thing.'

'Sometimes I don't understand either of my daughters,' Angela complained, 'but I suppose it is my own fault for bringing both of you up to be independent. Very well, darling, have it your own way.'

'How is Florence?' Lizzie asked after her sister.

'The last I heard she was organising a fresh water project somewhere in deepest Africa.'

'Good old Flo.' Lizzie smiled. 'I get the occasional e-mail, but you know her. She's never been one for paper-work. Unless she's knee-deep in dirt, she regards her day as wasted.'

Angela laughed with her daughter. There was a murmur of voices in the background. 'I've got to go. Don't forget I'm at the end of the phone if you need me.'

Lizzie returned her attention to her list of jobs to do. She supposed she would have to contact Steve's grand-mother. After yesterday's confrontation with Olivia's other grandson, there was no way Todd would endorse her decision for Lizzie to occupy one of the industrial park units, especially not when he discovered the beneficial terms of the contract Olivia proposed.

Lizzie's phone rang again.

'Lizzie? Charlie here.' Before she had a chance to return her greeting, Charlotte said, 'A man's been in the shop looking for you.'

'The same one as last night?' Lizzie asked in concern.

'No, this one gave his name. Todd Baxter. Unfortunately Alan was hang-ing around the back of the shop and he told this Mr Baxter that you rented our first floor flat before I could stop him.'

There was a loud knocking at the

door. 'That's all right, Charlie. No harm done.'

The buzzer was now being pressed with unnecessary vigour.

'Good morning.' Lizzie opened the door. 'If you've come looking for your brother then I have to tell you he isn't here. In fact, I still don't know where he is.'

'It would seem at last that we have something in common.' Todd was breathing heavily as if the effort of attacking her doorbell had been too much for him.

'I beg your pardon?'

Lizzie looked at Todd in confusion. Today he was wearing a blue shirt and casual denims. For the first time in months she felt the faintest flicker of attraction towards a man, before firmly reminding herself this was also a man who had accused her of using her feminine wiles on his brother in order to get her hands on a family inheritance.

'I've been on the telephone to Steve's office.'

'And you're here to deliver an apology for your accusations of last night?' Lizzie queried with her sweetest smile. 'How kind.'

'I'm not here to do anything of the sort.'

'You're not?' On her own ground and in the daylight Lizzie felt in a better position to challenge Todd. 'Then to what do I owe the pleasure of this visit?'

'I'm here to tell you Steve has not been seen in his office for several days now.'

'I fail to see what that has to do with me.'

Lizzie immediately regretted her flippancy, imagining how worried she would feel if Florence disappeared.

'Have you tried the health club?' she asked in a softer voice. 'Steve told me he was working on a contract for them and that was why he was probably going to be late for our meeting last night.'

'They haven't seen him, either. Are you sure you really don't know where he is?'

Lizzie held her door open wide. 'You are welcome to take a look round. There are very few places to hide, but I can assure you Steve's not here.'

Todd ran a distracted hand through his hair. It stood on end creating an air of vulnerability.

'Don't you realise that apart from my grandmother you would appear to be among one of the last people to have had contact with him?'

An Even Keel

Paul Owen sipped a cappuccino. The view from the golf club terrace always relaxed him. It was tiring work erecting marquees and this last week business had been brisk and the customers demanding. He had tried to persuade his father to let him take control of the business side of things but so far with no success. His father had insisted he needed hands on experience before settling to anything else.

'Once you've done all the dirty jobs,' he explained to his son, 'you'll be in a better position to understand the basics of the job and the problems that can arise.'

'You've let Mark develop the Devon contract.'

'That's because he's moved down there. It made sense. He also has a wife who is a steadying influence on him,' his father added with a significant glance.

Paul glared moodily into his empty coffee cup. Mark had always been the blue-eyed boy. Whatever he wanted seemed to drop into his lap. Even after that business with Lizzie he managed to sort out his personal life. His new wife was a lovely girl and Paul was envious of his brother's domestic harmony.

He looked down at his hands. One of his fingernails was damaged from where he had been careless with a hammer.

The daughter of the house whose garden they were getting ready for an eighteenth birthday party had smiled at him and his hand slipped.

If only his father would allow him more free time, Paul thought, he would have liked to invite the girl out. She was pretty and looked fun.

He glanced over to the car park. Two lady golfers were admiring his red convertible. A smile of satisfaction crossed Paul's face. The car had been a present from an elderly female relative who knew how to spoil him.

His parents were usually too busy to take time off during the day to visit her and now Mark had moved away it fell to Paul to keep an eye on their great aunt.

At least his father was grateful for that. Paul had hoped he would have a rethink about the amount of physical work his son was doing. If Paul wasn't erecting or dismantling a marquee, he was counting endless cups, saucers and spoons and stacking them appropriately.

It had been a stroke of luck seeing Lizzie's advert in that newsagents' window. One of their regulars had gone sick at the last moment and Paul had been called in to cover at short notice. He had only stopped by the shop to pick up a newspaper and there it was. *Lizzie Hilton*. If Paul closed his eyes he could visualise her ravishing red hair and sapphire blue eyes. The freckles on her nose danced when she smiled. The first time Paul had seen her it was as if a surge of electricity had passed through his veins.

It had been at the house of a family friend and she had been invited as Mark's guest. Even now Paul could remember his bitter disappointment when his brother had introduced them. Lizzie had been friendly and laughed politely at his jokes, but she'd only had eyes for Mark. Over the coming weeks Paul did everything in his power to win her away from him, but when that didn't work he started rumours about her background.

If only Lizzie had returned his feelings, none of the unpleasantness that followed would have occurred.

After she had disappeared out of his life he had done everything possible to find her again. He wanted to apologise and try to make amends, and now he had discovered her whereabouts he wasn't going to let her slip through his fingers a second time. His behaviour had done a lot of damage to her relationship with his family and he wanted to put things right.

She had turned him down once, but now she was no longer with Mark there was no reason for her to turn him down again.

Once he had proved to his parents that he was a willing worker and could be trusted to run a part of the family business he hoped they, too, would accept Lizzie back into the family fold. Unfortunately he had done such a good job blackening her character with his unfounded allegations that even his parents had believed his stories. He would have to tread carefully if he wanted them to believe she wasn't as black as he had painted her.

★　★　★

Lizzie lay back in the bath. Her feet ached from all the walking she had done. She squeezed soapy water out of her sponge and massaged her aching limbs.

Lizzie had put off thinking about

Todd and Steve all day. She very much doubted Steve had totally disappeared and put Todd's concern down to the over-reaction he seemed to experience every time his younger brother's name was mentioned.

So far she had heard nothing from him, apart from the damaging letter Todd had discovered at the cottage.

Lizzie twisted the hot water tap with her foot. The water had grown cold and thinking about Todd appeared to have lowered the temperature in the bath.

He had eventually reluctantly agreed that Lizzie could have had nothing to do with Steve's temporary disappearance.

'I am concerned for my grandmother's sake,' he explained when he had calmed down. 'Steve takes after our parents. They were adventurous people, always up for new experiences. They thought nothing of trekking off to the middle of nowhere.

'When they died in a boating accident, my grandmother became even more protective of Steve. He was always a bit wild. Monty, our grandfather was a restraining influence on him, but after he passed away, Olivia tended to spoil Steve, not always for his own good.'

Lizzie's sympathies were with Todd. She knew what it was like to have an adventurous sibling and while her sister travelled the world Lizzie had been the stay-at-home girl.

Todd cleared his throat. 'I may have been a little hasty in some of the things I said last night,' he apologised. 'You wouldn't have been the first female to have set her sights on Steve and I am afraid I jumped to the wrong conclusion.'

Lizzie decided to accept his words for the generous apology they were. It was silly to go on arguing forever, and if anything really had happened to Steve they might need to join forces.

'You have my word that my relationship with your brother was nothing to do with any inheritance,' Lizzie assured him.

'He was planning on setting up in a place of his own, wasn't he?'

'You didn't hear it from me,' Lizzie protested.

'I didn't,' Todd acknowledged.

'How did you find out what was going on?' she asked.

'Olivia may be getting on in years, but her hearing is razor sharp. Steve telephoned you one night from Maiden Farm?'

'He mentioned that your grand-mother was prowling around in the background.'

'She overheard bits of your conversa-tion and put two and two together.' Todd paused then added with a rueful smile, 'She also sang your praises and rather took me to task for my suspicions about you. I caught sight of one of your cards in the shop window downstairs.' He paused. 'You're an interior design consultant?'

Lizzie took a deep breath, deter-mined to clear the air between them. 'There's something else I have to tell you. In your absence your grandmother made arrangements for me to lease one of your industrial units.'

'She didn't mention anything about that.'

'I also suspect she didn't mention the finer details of our negotiations.'

'As long as you're operating within the terms of the lease I am prepared to accept my grandmother's decision.'

'Even when she makes her own rules?'

'What sort of rules are we talking about here?' Todd asked, an edge to his voice.

'The more than generous terms of my rental. I have a feeling Mrs Baxter might be guilty of overstepping her authority.'

'May I know the financial details?' Todd enquired.

When Lizzie named the exact sum involved, Todd, to his credit, kept his cool.

'She must have a very high regard for your integrity,' he replied smoothly.

'Of course I wouldn't dream of holding you to the contract.' Lizzie began searching through her paperwork.

Todd waved the paperwork away. 'I wouldn't dream of it. My grandmother does actually have the authority to make decisions of this nature. I won't renege on a deal signed in good faith.'

With a twinge of remorse Lizzie was beginning to recall her robust reaction to some of Todd's observations the previous evening.

'I suppose it's my turn to apologise now,' she admitted. 'Last night. I think I might have been a little blunt in my personal observations about your integrity. I tend to speak first then think afterwards,' Lizzie explained.

'It's a common failing of people with red hair,' Todd agreed.

The silence between them lengthened, as Todd looked deep into her eyes. Lizzie sensed a tell-tale blush beginning to colour the base of her neck.

'Your apology is unnecessary,' Todd spoke carefully. 'I was equally as blunt in my observations. Shall we call it quits and start again?'

His handshake was firm and inspired Lizzie with confidence.

'Er, was there anything else?' she asked as he displayed a reluctance to let go of her fingers, 'only I have a busy day ahead of me and I need to get on.'

'Of course,' Todd replied. 'Perhaps if you do hear from Steve you'd let my grandmother know?'

'I will.'

'And you can move into your unit whenever you like. My number is on a list of emergency contacts by the door but I'm often in the main office. I'll drop by in a day or two and see how you are getting on.'

After Todd left it had taken Lizzie a few moments to collect her scattered thoughts. She knew she should have been thinking about Steve and wondering exactly what he was up to and why he hadn't been in touch, but all she could think about was Todd and brown eyes that reminded her of melted toffee.

'Long Time, No See'

'So glad you managed to fix things up with Todd.' Olivia's voice was a hoarse rasp down the telephone line. 'That's why I'm calling, to make sure you're still talking to me. I understand you and my grandson had words? I don't know the details but I hope you gave him as good as you got?'

Olivia ground to a halt. Lizzie could hear her now holding her breath as she waited for her reply.

'Whatever happened between Todd and me was not your fault, so let's forget all about it,' Lizzie assured her.

'Brilliant.' Olivia now sounded her normal ebullient self. 'I praised your assets to the skies. I told Todd your on site presence would be a bonus to the industrial estate. We need a feminine touch. Todd came round to my way of thinking, eventually.' Olivia added after a pause, 'When are you going to move in?'

'Perhaps tomorrow?'

'Great stuff. I'll bake a cake. How old are you?'

'Twenty-three, why?'

'I only want to know how many candles to light.'

'It's not my birthday, Olivia.'

Images of activated sprinklers spraying water all over her fine fabrics went through Lizzie's mind. Much as she liked Olivia, she felt the older lady possessed an enthusiasm that would have to be curbed if they didn't want a disaster on their hands.

'This is going to be an un-birthday cake. Actually,' Olivia confessed, 'I'm not terribly good at baking cakes, I may have to buy one in, but never mind, it will be there by fair means or foul. Do you like coffee and walnut or are you a strawberry cream sort of girl?'

'Whatever,' Lizzie replied.

Olivia sounded quite excited as she said, 'I may actually be able to put a bit of business your way. I still have contacts in the theatre and they're always designing new sets. I'll do a lunch one day and set up some connections for you. Have you heard from Steve at all?' she finished in a quiet voice.

'No,' Lizzie admitted, ashamed to realise in all the excitement she hadn't given him a second thought. 'Haven't you?'

'Not a word. I know he's only been gone a few days and he's a grown man, but you do worry about loved ones.'

Lizzie bit down her annoyance. It wasn't her place to voice her opinion on inconsiderate grandsons, but in her opinion Steve was being thoughtless in the extreme.

'Has he done this sort of thing before?' she asked.

'Once or twice,' Olivia admitted.

'I promise if I do hear from Steve you'll be the first to know,' Lizzie assured Olivia.

Later in the morning Lizzie set out

for the retail park. She always enjoyed the drive through the rolling Dorset hills. The views across the valley swept over miles of surrounding countryside.

On summer days it wasn't unknown for severe mist to sweep in from the sea obscuring all vision, but today it was possible to see for miles. She passed the remains of a small Roman settlement. The history of the area had always fascinated her and although she wasn't local, she couldn't imagine living anywhere else.

Her mother and sister possessed the wanderlust genes in the family. Once Lizzie had left school in Brussels she had headed back across the Channel and settled first in college to study the history of tapestry and embroidery skills, then after she had gained her arts degree she'd moved down from London to the south coast.

The sea provided a welcome contrast to the cosmopolitan sophistication of Brussels where Lizzie had grown up and there was nothing she enjoyed more than being by the water. Mark had been part of the sailing set and a lot of their social life had centred on the sea.

After her broken engagement to Mark she had taken on the challenge of setting up in business on her own and Maiden Magna was proving ideal for her needs.

The hired van began its rattled descent down the hill towards the retail outlet, Lizzie's first port of call. Wishing she had taken more time out to inspect her unit Lizzie decided to order the minimum requirements until she had a better chance to organise her new premises.

After spending a busy morning arranging deliveries for the coming week, Lizzie's stomach began to remind her that she had forgotten to eat breakfast that morning. The fragrant smells of hot peppers, cheese and jacket potatoes wafted over from the bistro and proved too tempting for Lizzie to resist.

'Table for one?' the cheerful waitress greeted her. Lizzie settled in a corner window seat and studied the menu.

A shadow temporarily blocked the light from the window. Lizzie looked up to see a photographer with his lens trained on a shop opposite.

'What's going on?' she asked the waitress as she delivered Lizzie's baked potato to her table.

'First day opening. The new shop is specialising in lovely retro fashions.'

'Surely a new shop doesn't merit this amount of interest?' Lizzie waved her fork at the gathering journalists.

'Didn't you see the posters? There's been a mass of publicity in the media. They've got Pearl Mason to cut the ribbon.' The expression on the waitress's face suggested Lizzie ought to be suitably impressed. 'Her father's that horse-racing man, you know? Anyway he jets around the world and Pearl usually accompanies him. She's always on the front of all the gossip mags because she's so beautiful. Her father spoils her dreadfully. She's the apple of his eye.'

'Does she normally do this sort of thing?' Lizzie asked. 'Cut ribbons at store openings? I mean horses and fashion don't really go together, do they? And she can't need the money.'

'That's the strange thing,' the waitress agreed. 'As far as anyone can remember this is the first time she has allowed her name to be associated with a retail product. I suppose that's why there's been such a fuss. There she is now.'

Lizzie turned her head but it was impossible to spot anyone through the sea of reporters jostling for the best shot of the guest of honour.

'Sorry.' The waitress rushed over after Lizzie had signalled a third time for her bill. 'It's a bit of a madhouse here this afternoon. Did you see her?'

'The famous Pearl?' Lizzie smiled. 'I don't think so, but to be honest if I had I don't know that I would have recognised her.'

'Someone's left an early edition of the local paper on one of the other tables. There she is.' The waitress pointed to the headlines. 'Her picture is already in it.'

A pretty blonde girl dressed in a remarkably simple day dress was wielding a huge pair of scissors and smiling for the cameras.

Lizzie scanned the article more out of politeness than interest.

'Thank you.' She handed it back to the waitress with a smile then settled her bill.

Lizzie paused on the patio outside the bistro. Every table was still taken but most of the crowd had moved on. She caught a movement out of the corner of her eye and, turning, glimpsed a man hand in hand with a blonde-haired girl making their way towards a silver saloon parked on the pavement. It was Pearl Mason. As they reached the car her companion looked round furtively then opened the door and bundled her in before racing round to the driver's side of the vehicle. Revving the engine he drove off before Lizzie was actually sure what she had seen.

Although she had only met him a handful of times, the car driver bore a remarkable resemblance to Steve Baxter.

Lizzie headed back towards her van to make the journey home.

Glad to see an empty parking space by the newsagents, she quickly slotted her little van into the spot, then going round the back opened the doors and began retrieving her parcels.

'Hello, Lizzie.' A voice greeted her as she struggled to stand upright. 'Long time, no see. Would you like me to help you with those?'

Paul Owen put out a hand and relieved her of a bolt of curtain material.

'This way, isn't it?' he asked and began making his way towards the entrance to her flat.

A Face From The Past

'How did you find out where I was?' Lizzie panted after him.

'The young boy in the shop said they kept your spare key for emergencies and that I could wait upstairs for you if I liked.'

'You had no right to enter my premises without my permission.'

'I didn't,' Paul replied with a smug smile.

'You said Alan opened up for you.'

'I didn't go inside, scout's honour.' He saluted and put the shopping down on the hall floor and turned on a light. 'That's better. Now we can look at each other properly.'

Lizzie slammed shut the door with the back of her foot.

'I had hoped not to have to look at you again.'

'Strong words,' Paul reproached her.

'Can't we let bygones be bygones?'

'You broke up my engagement to your brother.'

'If you had really been right for each other he wouldn't have let go of you so easily, would he?'

Paul was working his charisma at full potential, but it was wasted on Lizzie. She had seen it in action too many times to be swayed by his brand of charm. Behind the smile lurked a deeper emotion that surfaced whenever Paul didn't get his own way.

'You did such an efficient job of blackening my character that your parents threatened to cut all contact with him if he went through with the marriage. I couldn't let that happen.'

'Things were said in the heat of the moment that perhaps would have been better left unsaid,' Paul admitted, 'but my parents would never have seen through their threat.'

'I want you to leave, please, now.'

'Mark's married. Did you know?'

'Yes, and I'm pleased for him. I'm

also pleased he has moved to Devon. Maybe that way he will have better luck than I did staying out of your life.'

'You're being very harsh, Lizzie.'

'After what you did to my character I have every reason to be.'

Paul held out his arms. 'Lizzie, let's not quarrel. As you quite rightly say, life moves on. I want us to start again, too. I can understand how surprised you must be to see me again, but I assure you I'm only interested in your well-being. I'm sorry if my past behaviour upset you and I am here to make amends.'

'Why?' Lizzie demanded.

'Isn't it obvious?'

'Not to me.'

'The truth is I was jealous of Mark.'

'So jealous you circulated untrue stories about me? Stories that found their way into the local newspaper?'

'That was unfortunate, I agree. I had no idea that the man I was chatting to at the golf club was a reporter.'

'When I rang up the newspaper to

protest they told me they had paid you a handsome fee, so forgive me if your apologies don't ring true.'

A look of annoyance crossed Paul's face.

'Checking up on me, were you?'

'With good reason. Now will you leave?'

'You must be hungry after your day out. Why don't we have dinner together?'

Lizzie's jacket potato churned in her stomach.

'Have you got another date, is that it?' Paul's eyes darkened suspiciously.

'There's been no-one in my life since Mark.'

'Yes, you were always annoyingly loyal, weren't you?'

'Which is more than can be said of you.'

'I don't know what you mean.'

'While you were pressing your unwanted attentions on me you had a girlfriend.'

'Is that what this is all about?' Paul's

confident smile was back in place. 'Jealousy? From now on you're the only girl for me.'

His self-confidence temporarily rendered Lizzie speechless. She could not believe what she was hearing. It would seem Paul really believed she cared about him.

He picked up one of her leaflets off the table. 'Setting up on your own? Maybe I could help. In my line of business I come into contact with lots of people. Why don't I take a supply of these and distribute them for you?'

'I don't need your help.'

'We could all do with a little help from time to time. Maiden Magna?' Paul chuckled. 'Who would have thought you would wind up in a backwater like this?'

'What I do with my life is absolutely no business of yours.' Lizzie grabbed out at the leaflet Paul was still clutching.

A shadow of annoyance crossed his face.

'You needn't think I'm going to leave things like this.'

'You'd better if you know what's good for you. You were lucky I didn't take things further last time,' Lizzie returned the challenge.

'What do you mean?' Paul faltered.

'You made unfounded allegations about me. Things that weren't true were printed in the press.'

'The reporter misinterpreted my comments.'

'I don't believe you,' Lizzie replied.

It was a strong statement and had taken a lot of courage to blurt it out, but Paul Owen had almost ruined her life. She couldn't let it happen again.

The ringing of her mobile created a welcome break in the tension.

She turned away to take the call.

'Lizzie?'

'Hello, er, hello.'

With a sinking heart she recognised Todd Baxter's voice.

'Is something wrong?'

'No, why should there be?' she asked nervously.

'I'm checking to see if you've had any word from Steve?'

'No, I haven't.'

'I've tried his mobile and left countless messages hoping he'll get back to me. Olivia said she spoke to you this morning?'

'Yes. Does the name Pearl Mason mean anything to you?'

Lizzie caught a movement behind her. She glanced at Paul.

'Should it?' Todd asked.

'No reason. I thought I caught a glimpse of her today, that's all.'

'Who is this Pearl Mason?' Todd demanded.

'She was opening a shop in the retail park.'

'I still fail to see the connection to Steve.'

'They looked about the same age and it went through my mind maybe they were connected?'

It was a weak explanation but the

best Lizzie could come up with at short notice.

'You think he's gone off with her?'

'I didn't say that.'

Aware that she was getting in deeper and that Paul was listening to every word she said, Lizzie began to wish she had never mentioned Pearl's name to Todd.

'I only wish he'd told me what he was up to.'

'You don't think anything serious has happened to him?'

'Like an accident, you mean? No,' Todd dismissed her suggestion. 'I didn't tell Olivia but I contacted one of Steve's old girlfriends and she told me she was driving by a sports shop and saw him inside and she thought he was trying on a riding hat.'

Lizzie caught her breath. The waitress at lunchtime had mentioned Pearl's father was involved in the world of horse-racing.

'Does Steve ride?' she asked.

'He's scared stiff of horses ever since

he fell off as a boy. Anyway, it's not your problem.' There was a pause before Todd asked 'Olivia mentioned something about baking a cake to celebrate your arrival?'

'That's right. She did.'

'I think I should warn you her baking skills aren't one of her strengths. Anyway, when are you moving in?'

'I haven't exactly made up my mind yet. Can I call you back?' Lizzie did her best to keep the tone of her voice neutral.

'You've got my number? Keep in touch.'

'What was all that about Pearl Mason?' Paul asked as Lizzie ended the call.

'Do you know her?'

'Only by reputation.'

'Who was that on the phone?'

'My calls are private, Paul.'

Before she could stop him he grabbed up her telephone and pressing the last number recall button listened to a recorded message.

'Todd Baxter? Would that be *the* Todd Baxter, the one who runs the industrial park? Don't bother to deny it. I can see by your face it is. You know for a moment there I really believed you when you said you were going solo.'

'I am, now will you please leave?'

'Don't worry. I'm going but you haven't heard the last of me. As for Todd Baxter, I expect he would be interested to learn of your past, wouldn't he?'

'I haven't got a past.'

Paul's smile was as warm as ice.

'Maybe not, but that newspaper story would make for interesting reading, wouldn't you say?'

'It wasn't true.'

'He's not to know that is he? And I don't expect you've told him that your previous engagement was broken off because the family suspected you were after Mark's money?'

'Why are you doing all this?' Lizzie demanded.

'I don't like being made to look a

fool,' Paul replied.

'I've never made you look foolish.'

'You made your feelings for me perfectly clear when I offered to console you after the break-up of your engagement. Now if you were to rethink those feelings, perhaps I could be persuaded not to contact your new boyfriend.'

At the height of all the upset Lizzie's mother had suggested they take legal action against Paul, but Lizzie had only wanted out of the situation and it had been her choice to make a new life for herself.

Now the consequences did not bear thinking about. Should Paul show the press cuttings to Todd he would probably start believing she really was involved in Steve's disappearance and that Pearl Mason was nothing more than a smokescreen.

'Nothing to say?' Paul taunted her.

Lizzie tossed back her head.

'You must do what you like,' she flashed back at him, determined to stand her ground.

'Don't you realise how foolish you're being?'

'Perhaps, but I can't keep running away from you for ever. If you choose to blacken my name then there's nothing I can do to stop you, but I should warn you to tread carefully.'

'Or you'll do what?'

'My mother has influential connections. I declined her help last time. Now I might take up her offer.'

'You haven't heard the last of this,' Paul retaliated.

Lizzie listened to his footsteps retreating down the stairs. She was quaking in every limb.

A Welcome Party

As Lizzie negotiated the drive leading to the industrial park she could hear loud music blaring, not the radio type of music she would have expected from the garage mechanics, but a full-blown brass band.

She had spent a leisurely morning sorting out her boxes of samples, labelling everything and waiting for the carrier to collect the bulkier items she couldn't transport herself. Then she had laden up her trusty van and set out with not exactly a song in her heart but feeling more optimistic about the future.

The road now curved to the right and as Lizzie negotiated the bend she saw to her amazement several helium balloons buffeting against a crudely decorated banner that judging from the precarious nature of the structure, had been hastily erected across the, main entrance. Any moment now the balloons looked as though they might work loose from their moorings and take flight.

'*Welcome to Maiden Farm, Lizzie,*' she read the multicoloured printed message aloud.

'There she is,' she heard a throaty voice boom in the background during a lull in the music.

The next moment the brass band broke into a spirited version of 'Happy Days Are Here Again'. Several couples began dancing on a patch of lawn. Other people stood around whooping and clapping.

As Lizzie began to wonder if she had driven through the looking glass her driver's door was yanked open by Olivia, who was wearing an outrageous wedding hat and a chiffon ensemble more suited to a garden party that an oily industrial estate.

'Party time,' Olivia announced. 'Out you get. Will one of you lovely gentlemen park the lady's van for her?'

A sea of volunteers swarmed forward.

'Hi, allow me. I'm Jack.' A boiler-suited man jumped into the driving seat Lizzie had recently vacated.

'Trust you to get to the lady first,' another male grumbled in the background. 'It's always the same with him.' He beamed at Lizzie. 'My name's Alf and I am a much better driver.'

'He's also much older,' Jack retaliated, then frowned as he tried to re-start the van. 'You need a new battery, Lizzie, this one's almost flat.'

'I do the best deals in batteries,' another eager male pushed forward.

'Gentlemen, please stop squabbling.' Olivia took charge of the situation. 'I'll introduce you all later, but right now, Lizzie, you have to come and inspect your unit.'

'Do you welcome all your newcomers like this?' Lizzie managed to gasp before Olivia grabbed her elbow.

'Only the ones I like. This way.'

Before Lizzie could protest further

she was frogmarched towards her breezeblock unit.

Olivia threw open the door. In the middle of the table stood a three-tiered cake, iced in pink and loaded with candles. On a side table was a stack of cards and several brightly wrapped presents.

'You shouldn't have gone to so much trouble.'

'Todd's been called away so I decided it was time we had a unit social gathering and what better occasion than to welcome our first lady to the fold?'

'Todd's not here?' Lizzie couldn't resist looking over her shoulder to double check he hadn't sneaked up on them without warning.

'Nope. He may be back later but I thought if I told him of my plans in advance he might make objections. He can be a bit of a party pooper, so I didn't tell him.'

'Olivia,' Lizzie chided, 'you shouldn't do this sort of thing. You know it annoys Todd.'

'Yes, I should. I love a party. Monty and I were renowned for our bashes in the past and the lads were really up for it, too. We all need to let our hair down every now and then. Come on outside and meet the gang.'

The sea of faces greeting her was friendly and everyone was keen to make her acquaintance.

'Good news.' Olivia beamed from under her hat, the brim of which was now skew whiff. She waved a slice of salmon quiche at Lizzie. 'I've heard from Steve.'

'You've heard from Steve?' Lizzie raised her voice above the hubbub going on around them.

'Sssh.' Olivia shushed her. 'We don't want anyone to overhear.'

'Why not?'

'It's hush hush, and we're not to mention anything to Todd. Steve said to tell you he's fine and he'll be back as soon as he can, and he still wants you to go ahead with the job. Here.' Olivia pulled a piece of paper out of her pocket. 'This is for you. It's a retainer.'

Lizzie glanced down at the crumpled cheque Olivia thrust at her.

'I can't accept this. It's far too much.'

'Course you can, and before you start accusing me of being over-generous, it was Steve's idea, so if you have any complaints, I suggest you take them up with him.'

'Didn't he give you any idea when he would be back?'

'To be honest, darling, it was a bit of a crackly line and I couldn't catch absolutely all he was saying, but I was so pleased to hear from him everything else went by the board.' Olivia grabbed at her hat as a vigorous gust of wind threatened to dislodge it. 'I suspect there's a girlfriend involved somewhere along the line. Did I tell you I came across him and a young lady one evening in his sitting room? Anyway, she looked extremely at home'

'You don't happen to remember her name, do you?' Lizzie asked, wondering if her initial suspicions about Steve and

Pearl Mason were true.

'No,' Olivia replied. 'She and I had a lovely time talking about horses. Monty used to follow the racing on the television whenever he got the chance.'

Olivia then drifted off.

'I presume all this is in your honour?'

Lizzie didn't have to turn round to know that Todd Baxter was standing behind her.

'What's wrong with it?' she demanded, loyalty to his grandmother forbidding her from mentioning Olivia as the instigator.

'Nothing at all, except I'm not sure holding a party falls within the terms of the lease.'

'There must be times when they can be overridden?'

The expression on his face softened into a resigned smile.

'I suppose that like Olivia, you belong to the 'rules are flexible,' movement?'

'If it doesn't do any harm, yes.'

'Would you like to dance?'

The question took Lizzie by surprise.

'What was that?'

'I asked you if you'd like to dance.'

Todd moved in closer and in one fluid movement he slipped his arm around her waist. Lizzie froze as his deep brown eyes worked their magic on her.

'I knew my sessions at Miss McFadden's academy would come in useful one day. Mind those oil drums,' he murmured in Lizzie's ear, 'and watch out for any stray nuts and bolts.'

'What are you doing?' Lizzie demanded, regaining her senses as Todd steered her expertly through the minefield of debris littering the ground beneath their feet.

'I'm not too sure of the technical term, but I think it's something between a quick step and a waltz.'

'Everyone's looking at us,' Lizzie protested.

'Only because you're making a fuss.'

'I am not making a fuss.'

'Good,' Todd whispered into her ear. 'In that case let's give it another twirl.'

Todd turned out to be a more than

adequate dancer, guiding Lizzie through all the moves in time to the music as it turned into a slow number.

Lizzie knew she was breathing heavily, but there was nothing she could do about it. She also suspected her colour had risen.

'I am supposed to be moving in to my unit, not tripping the light fantastic with the management.'

'Now is not the time to worry about logistics, but I think you owe it to my grandmother to look as though you are enjoying her party. I went to great pains to pretend I knew nothing about it.'

'You knew of her plans?'

'Olivia has many fine qualities but arranging a party in secret is not one of them.' A smile tugged at the corner of Todd's mouth. 'For the past week she has been giving out this number to everyone telling them to drop by any time during the afternoon. I can't count the number of calls I have received accepting her kind invitation.'

Reluctant amusement bubbled up in

Lizzie's chest, until she found she was laughing aloud.

'I don't think,' she managed to say, 'I've ever met such a peculiar family.'

'I agree,' Todd said mock seriously. 'We are a bit of a handful, but that's what families are all about, isn't it? Rubbing along together despite their eccentricities. So welcome to the family of Maiden Farm.'

Before Lizzie realised his intention Todd again curved his arms around her waist and kissed her gently on the cheek.

'There,' he said. 'The deal has been properly sealed, wouldn't you say?'

He turned and walked off to join the clutch of mechanics still gathered round the buffet.

A Mystery Is Solved

'Still here?' The flash of a torch made Lizzie jump. 'Sorry, didn't mean to startle you. How's it going?'

'I didn't realise it was so late,' Lizzie replied with a smile. 'Think I'm about finished.'

'I must say you've made it very comfortable.' The security guard looked round approvingly. 'A home from home.'

'That was the idea,' Lizzie explained. 'I want my unit to be a showcase of what can be done on a budget. If people want to see how a particular colour scheme works or what a pattern looks like made up, I can show them one of my examples.'

'Best be on my way. Don't forget to lock up before you leave.'

Lizzie hummed to herself as she tidied up then padlocked the outer doors — something the insurance company insisted on.

Lizzie had been based at the business park for a week now. The relationship between her and Todd had settled into a comfortable routine of sharing a coffee together if either of them were available. The first time Todd had knocked on her door she had been engrossed in some fine stitching and his arrival had taken her by surprise.

'Like to do my daily rounds,' he explained, 'make sure there are no outstanding issues.'

He sniffed appreciatively.

'Fresh ground Colombian coffee.' Lizzie offered. 'I've home-baked cookies, too, if you're interested.'

'A businesswoman who bakes her own cookies?' Todd smiled. 'Will you marry me?'

'I hate to disappoint you . . . ' Lizzie poured out two mugs, 'but my landlady's daughter made the cookies. Cherry and almond or walnut crunch?'

A warm breeze had wafted through

Lizzie's open doors easing away the tension in the back of her neck. Although Steve was still away Lizzie suspected Olivia had hinted to Todd that there was no need to worry about him.

Lizzie, too, had taken into dropping by Todd's office. His unit was a little larger than the others and furnished with more business machines. Until she first visited his office Lizzie had not realised quite how comprehensive an operation he ran. The telephones rang constantly in the background; a fax rattled away in a far corner and two computers were busy backing up data.

'Is it always this busy?' she managed to ask during a lull in activity.

'I used to have an assistant, but she's on maternity leave. I didn't get round to arranging temporary cover and now I don't think she's coming back,' Todd explained. 'I'll have to do something about it, but it's finding the time.'

'I'll help if you like,' Lizzie volunteered.

'If you're sure?'

Todd produced a file of letters that needed to be sent and showed her which computer to use.

Some evenings Todd's light was still on when she left work, but tonight it was in darkness. Lizzie wondered briefly if he had much of a social life. Olivia had mentioned a brief broken engagement a few years earlier, but ever since Lizzie had been working at the Maiden Farm estate there had been no evidence of a regular female companion.

There had been no further contact from Paul Owen, for which Lizzie was grateful.

There were no messages on her telephone when Lizzie arrived back at her flat. She bit down her disappointment. Whilst she enjoyed working for Todd she really needed to get back on the road to do a bit more self-promotion. Mentally making a note to mention her plans to Todd the next day she heated up some soup.

It was on evenings like this she missed company. Mark had enjoyed a busy social schedule and they were often out every night of the week. It was at times exhausting and Lizzie used to long for a quiet night in. Now the reverse was true.

The ringing of the telephone disturbed Lizzie from her paperwork.

Flicking off the television she picked up the receiver.

'Is that Lizzie Hilton?' a female asked in an uncertain voice.

'Yes.'

'The interior designer?'

'That's right. Can I help you?'

'My name is Pearl Mason.'

Lizzie nearly dropped the receiver.

'Did you say Pearl Mason?' She repeated the name clearly.

'You've heard of me?' the caller asked in a world-weary voice.

'Not really, I mean, I thought I saw you the other day.'

'Steve said he thought it was you.'

'Steve Baxter?'

'Yes, he's the reason I'm calling.'

'I'm sorry,' Lizzie apologised. 'I don't understand.'

'How well do you know Steve?' The suspicious note was back in Pearl's voice.

'Hardly at all. We had an appointment to meet in Wrenn Close but he never appeared. That was over two weeks ago.'

'He's very sorry about that, but he said he left you a letter in the cottage. Didn't you get it?'

'Eventually, after his brother Todd read it and accused me and Steve of conducting a romantic liaison.'

'Todd did what?'

'He also inferred I wanted to get my hands on the family inheritance.'

'Goodness.' Pearl sounded genuinely shocked. 'That's quite some accusation.'

'Exactly, so you'll understand how I feel about Steve Baxter.'

'You've got him all wrong.'

'Have I? His poor grandmother has

been worried about him, too.'

'He has contacted her.'

'So I believe.' Lizzie hesitated. 'Was there something else?'

'Can we meet up? I could come round now.'

'Where are you?' Lizzie asked.

'I don't want to talk on the telephone. I'll be with you in fifteen minutes, if that's convenient?'

'Do we have to be quite so theatrical?' Lizzie enquired.

'Believe me,' Pearl assured her. 'We do.'

Lizzie tidied up her papers then looked out of the window to see a shadowy figure making its furtive way down the street. She could tell the figure was female from her slender build.

The doorbell buzzed. Lizzie opened it. She had only seen one smudged newspaper photograph of Pearl Mason but she had to admit she was one of the most beautiful females she had ever seen in her life.

'Can I come in?' she asked in a whispery voice. 'I feel a bit exposed out here.' Without waiting for Lizzie's permission she sidled into the living-room. 'Reporters have a nasty habit of following me around.'

Lizzie poked her head out the door. The street outside was deserted and, as far as she could ascertain, devoid of paparazzi.

'Would you like some refreshment?'

Pearl shrugged off her jacket. Underneath she was wearing a pink cashmere sweater, pearls and the smartest designer jeans Lizzie had ever seen in her life.

'No, thank you,' Pearl replied, tucking a stray strand of blonde hair into her black velvet Alice band. 'You must be wondering what on earth I am doing here?'

'The thought had crossed my mind,' Lizzie admitted.

'It's difficult to know where to start.' Pearl perched on the edge of the sofa. 'Why don't you make yourself at home and tell me what this is all about?' Lizzie suggested.

'Steve Baxter and I are an item,' Pearl admitted. 'Actually, we're a bit more than that.'

'Go on,' Lizzie urged.

'My father is very possessive.' Pearl looked questioningly at Lizzie as if she were expecting some input. 'Giles Mason?' she prompted.

'The waitress in the snack bar told me about him. I gather he's quite important in the horse-racing circles.'

Pearl nodded.

'We are very close. After my parents separated and my mother moved to South America it was decided I would stay with my father and his unmarried sister in order not to disrupt my schooling. My aunt married when I was sixteen and after that we've always done everything together, but lately, well, I met Steve at evening classes.'

'Don't tell me you were studying woodwork,' Lizzie joked.

'Actually I was.'

If the sky had fallen in Lizzie could not have been more surprised.

'I'm quite good with my hands.' Pearl blushed. 'I thought it would be fun to do something that had no connection with horses. Dad goes out with the boys on a Wednesday so I took up woodwork. Steve was standing in for the tutor who'd gone sick and it was love at first sight.' she giggled. 'He made me a sweet little rose turned box. It's so delicate. I keep it on my dressing table. The thing is,' the anxious look had returned to Pearl's face, 'my father likes to vet all my boyfriends.'

'And you don't think he would approve of Steve?'

'I don't know if he would or wouldn't, but I don't want to run the risk. That's why we took to meeting up in secret. We tried to get together once or twice at Maiden Farm.' Pearl tweaked at a speck of dirt on her jumper. 'Have you met Olivia?'

'I have,' Lizzie acknowledged with a wry smile.

'Steve started to get a bit annoyed when she kept dropping in on us of an evening. That was what decided him to get a place of his own. Somewhere we could meet up undisturbed by his grandmother or my father.'

'Number six, Wrenn Close?'

Pearl nodded.

'Where is Steve anyway?' Lizzie demanded, annoyed that yet again he had landed her in a situation not of her own making. 'Why isn't he here?'

'Because he's in traction.'

'What?'

'He's fractured a bone in his leg. I was teaching him to ride and he fell off. We thought it might impress my father if he knew how to handle a horse. Steve is a bit nervous around horses so we picked the gentlest mount in the stable, but she was feeling frisky and Steve panicked.'

A fleeting memory of someone mentioning having seen Steve in a sports shop passed through Lizzie's mind.

'It's not a serious fracture but it has delayed our plans.'

'What plans would they be?'

'To move into Wrenn Close — eventually. You see we want to get married.'

Keeping A Secret

Jessie Price's house was surrounded by beautifully landscaped gardens. She was standing on the steps of an imposing set of steps, flanked by stone statues of guard dogs and looking every inch the lady of the manor.

'So pleased to meet you, dear.'

She kissed Lizzie on the cheek.

'Any friend of Olivia's,' she trilled, 'is a friend of mine and I feel I know you already. I'm sorry I missed her party. Unfortunately her invitation clashed with Danny whisking me away to Paris for the weekend. He's such a romantic.'

A young man hovered at Jessie's elbow.

'There you are. Perhaps you'd carry Miss Hilton's bags for her, Rick? We'll have coffee in the conservatory, shall we?'

'Thank you, Mrs Price.'

'Jessie, please. It's actually Miss Price, but I only use that name for professional purposes. I'm really Mrs Winter. The problems of being an actress.' She laughed. 'So many names. Now, come on through.'

The gardens at the back of the house were even more impressive than those at the front.

'We love living here,' Jessie explained, 'Danny and I, that's Mr Winter, my husband. He sends his apologies by the way. He couldn't be here today to meet you because he's been called away. Someone's been taken ill and he's had to stand in on a breakfast chat show. They sent a car, which was most convenient, as he had to be at the studio at the crack of dawn. These days, now the acting work has dried up, we take anything that's offered. Someone has to pay for the upkeep of this place and we couldn't bear to move.'

'I can understand.' Lizzie sipped her fragrant coffee.

'When Olivia told me about your

exclusive services I pounced. I mean I know you're outrageously busy. Olivia said she doubted you'd be able to fit me into your schedule as your order book is bulging, but I pleaded with her to see if you could find a window.'

Lizzie did her best not to splutter. Olivia was nothing if not inventive. Still, Lizzie thought, it would do her reputation no disservice to let her clients think she was heavily in demand.

'Olivia mentioned new curtains.' she managed to say in a steady voice.

'That's right, for the drawing room. It's Danny's birthday, and I'm giving the dear old boy a party as a present and I told him I absolutely refuse to receive guests with those dreadful drapes on display.'

'Have you any ideas what you are looking for?'

'Masses, darling. I'll have to be restrained because I always go totally over the top. We're hoping for good weather then we can boot everyone out into the garden, and they might not notice the furnishings, but it's as well to be prepared, don't you think? In case we have to abandon the great outdoors?'

'Perhaps I ought to take a look?' Lizzie retrieved her notebook from her capacious satchel.

'Right, well, if you've finished your coffee, follow me.'

Jessie's heels clicked over the parquet flooring. She was a petite woman but with an actress's instinct, she knew how to disguise her lack of height by moving well.

'They're very large.' Lizzie inspected the curtains that were currently drawn open to reveal French windows leading down to the terrace.

'Exactly and you can see what an eyesore they are.'

'When is your party?' Lizzie asked.

'At the end of the month.'

'That doesn't give us much time.'

'I'm quite prepared to agree terms today and of course I'll pay a supplement for your trouble. Please say you can help out?' she pleaded.

'Why don't you look at my samples?' Lizzie suggested, 'Whilst I work out measurements and calculate costs?'

Jessie settled down on the sofa and began happily going through Lizzie's books.

'I rather like this material,' Jessie said, holding up a rich velvet fabric. 'What do you think?'

'It would work with your colour scheme,' Lizzie agreed.

'I suppose I've picked the most expensive example?'

'One of them.'

⋆ ⋆ ⋆

'I am so excited you would not believe.' Jessie helped Lizzie repack her bags after they shook hands on their deal. 'You absolutely must come to the party. Danny is so looking forward to meeting you. You haven't met Stephanie, have you?'

'I don't think I have.'

'She's from Danny's side of the family. That grandson of Olivia's broke her heart so she ran off to America.'

'That sounds like Steve,' Lizzie agreed.

'Anyway she's over all that now. She's married to a lovely husband.' Jessie paused. 'But it wasn't Steve who broke her heart, dear.'

'It wasn't?'

'No, it was Todd.' Jessie gave a light laugh. 'Still, mustn't gossip. Now back to business,' she gushed.

In a daze and not quite able to believe what Jessie had told her, Lizzie followed the older woman back into the conservatory where Jessie wrote out a cheque for the full agreed amount.

'I haven't presented you with a bill,' Lizzie protested doing her best to be businesslike, 'or a contract.'

'Send it through when you have time.' Jessie brushed aside her concern. 'I've found if you settle bills quickly you get a good level of service and I never get round to paperwork when dealing with people I trust. It drives my accountant mad.'

'I'm certain the party will be a great success,' Lizzie reassured her, doing her best not to think about Todd's affair with Stephanie.

'You've another visitor, Jessie,' Rick announced from the doorway.

'How very tiresome.' Jessie sighed. 'I need to get everything done in a hurry while Danny's out of the way, but it does put me under pressure. Can I leave you to find your own way out, dear?'

'I'd like to wander around to get the feel of things, Jessie. If that's all right with you.'

'Of course it is. Go wherever you like.'

She wafted away and Lizzie strolled out on to the terrace. Over the past week the weather had warmed up and she had received several enquiries regarding new commissions. By far the most prestigious had been Jessie's. As promised Olivia had thrown an all day party and people had drifted in and out of Maiden Farm, most of them pleased to accept one of Lizzie's flyers.

While Lizzie had been circulating, the gossip had flown thick and fast. As she was working the room she caught a passing reference to Pearl Mason.

'I have heard,' a partygoer lowered her voice, 'that there's a new boyfriend.'

'Does he meet with her father's approval?' another voice joined in.

'Do they ever?'

The laughter that followed this remark convinced Lizzie that Steve's choice to lie low had been a wise decision.

Pearl told Lizzie that while his leg was healing Steve was staying in a discreet hotel, the location of which almost amounted to a state secret. When all the necessary paperwork had been seen to, Steve and Pearl intended to get married quietly before telling her father. They also eventually intended to make their permanent base at Wrenn Close.

'That's why I'm here,' Pearl explained. 'Steve didn't want you to think he'd lost interest, but for the moment we have to put our plans on hold.'

'Where are you staying?' Lizzie asked Pearl.

'My father's away on business, so I'm using one of his company flats. It's quite convenient for seeing Steve and he's able to do a little freelance architectural work while he's convalescing.'

By the end of Pearl's visit, Lizzie's head reeled from the subterfuge and counter subterfuge going on in her life. All that concerned Lizzie was that Steve was paying her a retainer to keep his job on the back burner. Any further confidences she did not need and she had told Pearl quite firmly that she didn't want to hear any more of her secrets.

Lizzie stood in the centre of Jessie's lawn admiring the view. It was an idyllic spot and Lizzie understood Jessie and Danny's reluctance to leave.

A contractor was mowing the grass in the paddock and another was tending to the formal flower-beds. The background buzzed with activity.

'Fancy seeing you here.'

Lizzie squinted at the man standing in front of her. In the afternoon sunlight Paul Owen's eyes seemed bluer than ever.

Further Confrontation

A confident smile crossed his face. 'It seems chance has thrown us into each other's company. I couldn't have planned things better myself.'

Lizzie was doing her best to gather her scattered wits. The last person she had expected to see here was Paul Owen.

'I heard old Jessie doing her prima donna stuff about the curtains while I was waiting in the hall. She's quite a lady, isn't she?'

'Why are you here?' Lizzie demanded.

Paul's smile still tugged the corner of his mouth. 'I'm doing the quotes for the marquee and Jessie accepted our offer on the spot. It seems that's the way she likes to do things. She wants the works and a full team of helpers to set things up. She'll be keeping us busy for several weeks. We'll have to pull out all the stops.'

The brightness of the sun was beginning to stab Lizzie's eyes. 'If you'll excuse me.' Lizzie shielded her eyes from the sun and moved away from Paul. 'I have to get on.'

'You're not leaving on my account, I hope?'

Paul put out a hand to detain her. A sly look crossed his face.

'A little bird tells me you were being economical with the truth the other day.'

'Paul, I've no idea what you're talking about.'

'I'm talking about you and Steve Baxter.'

'There is no me and Steve Baxter. Your little bird got its wires crossed.' Lizzie raised her chin in challenge.

'So it's his brother Todd, is it?'

'It's not him, either.' Lizzie shook his hand off her arm.

Paul appeared not to have heard her reply. 'I have to hand it to you. The Baxters are one up on the Owens. Don't the boys inherit a packet on marriage?'

'I really wouldn't know. Steve Baxter is a prospective business contact nothing more.'

'You know,' Paul's voice was now silky soft, 'with Mark off the scene there's nothing to stop us getting together.'

'Why can't you leave me alone?'

'You don't really mean that, do you?'

He strolled away, leaving Lizzie standing alone in the middle of the lawn.

If only she hadn't already agreed things with Jessie she could have renegotiated the contract to make sure her visits didn't coincide with Paul's, but there was no way Lizzie was going back on a deal. Her professional reputation would suffer and Jessie would have every right to be outraged.

Paul Owen was not going to threaten her a second time and it was important to think things through carefully and not do anything rash.

By Lizzie's reckoning the marquee would be erected during the week running up to the party. Her work should be finished by then. It would mean several round-the-clock sessions, but it wouldn't be the first time she'd done that sort of thing and if it meant not bumping into Paul Owen, it was worth the inconvenience and effort.

She didn't doubt Paul was capable of making her life difficult if he thought she was involved with either Steve or Todd, and with Steve now secretly engaged to Pearl Mason, unwanted publicity would be the last thing the family would want.

As for Todd, would he believe Paul's scurrilous stories about her? If the mood took him she didn't doubt Paul wouldn't hesitate to show Todd a copy of that wretched newspaper interview.

Lizzie hurried across the grass to her van. There was no sign of Paul's car in the drive but a strong smell of exhaust fumes bore evidence of his recent departure. She hoped that given time and her lack of encouragement he would give up on the idea of their getting together.

Lizzie spent the remainder of the afternoon making preliminary sketches for Jessie's curtains. It would make sense she thought, to carry out the assignment in her lock up. She could work with the doors open and that would give her plenty of room to manoeuvre.

Geared up with enthusiasm now the job was underway, Lizzie drove over to Maiden Farm. Todd beckoned her over from his office window.

'We've got a bit of a rush job on. Do you think you could do some overtime tonight? I'll pay you a bonus, double your normal rate, with a takeaway pizza thrown in?' he coaxed.

'Cream cheese, smoked salmon and cracked black pepper?' Lizzie named the most expensive choice on the menu Todd had thrust under her nose.

'You're on.' His face split into his craggy smile.

He wasn't as handsome as Steve, but his eyes drew Lizzie into their warmth.

She wanted to straighten the collar of his crumpled work shirt, but she quelled such a gesture of intimacy. Todd was only smiling at her because he needed her help. Besides, hadn't Jessie told her he'd broken Stephanie's heart? There might have been an element of exaggeration in what she had said, but when it came to the Baxters it was as well to remember they had the power to hurt you.

'How late will I be?' Lizzie asked, getting her thoughts back on track.

Todd frowned.

'Stupid of me. I should have thought. You've probably got plans for this evening.' The hopeful look on his face faded quickly.

'No,' Lizzie assured him. 'This evening's fine, as long as I don't get into trouble with security for working late.'

'I'll tell them, don't worry about that. I would stay with you and help but Olivia wants me to drive her out to visit one of her friends. She doesn't like driving at night and it's a long-standing invitation. Steve normally does the honours on these occasions.' Todd paused. 'You haven't heard from him, have you?'

'Not exactly,' Lizzie hesitated, 'but his latest lady friend contacted me.'

'What's he playing at?' Todd raised his eyebrows in disbelief. 'He's not in any sort of trouble, is he?'

'He's fine.'

If Todd hadn't been looking at her so intently Lizzie would have crossed her fingers. It was only a white lie. According to Pearl, Steve's leg was on the mend but Todd might not see things in the same light.

'Why does he always have to lead such a complicated life?' Todd's jaw stiffened. 'What's she like this female?'

'Um, well, she's young and blonde.'

'Why didn't Steve get in touch with you himself?'

'He had his reasons,' Lizzie improvised. 'He felt bad about letting me down that night at Wrenn Cottage. She

126

came to my flat to offer his apologies.'

'That's typical of my brother, getting someone else to do his dirty work.'

'You're being a bit harsh on him.'

'Am I?' A frown knotted Todd's eyebrows. 'It's always been the same. Olivia goes soft on him because he's the baby of the family and I've always had to pick up the pieces afterwards. This time he's gone too far.'

'I'm sure he'll be in touch with you soon.'

'He'll get a piece of my mind when he does reappear. It's time he grew up.' Todd glared at Lizzie. 'Why do I get the feeling there's something you're not telling me?' His eyes were alight with suspicion.

'I've told you as much as I can,' Lizzie insisted. 'Perhaps Olivia can fill you in on the details.'

'I don't like mentioning Steve's name to her,' Todd's voice was less of an accusation now, 'she worries about him.'

'If he gets in touch again I'll try to

persuade him to talk to you.'

'Sorry,' Todd apologised, 'you're right, our family problems aren't your business. Are you still on for tonight?' He changed the subject. 'I'll make sure the office is heated and I'll order your takeaway for nine o'clock. I wouldn't want you fainting from hunger.'

Lizzie eyed the pile of work Todd had laid out for her.

'It looks worse than it is,' he assured her.

'I'll take your word for it.'

'Sorry I can't treat you to a better meal, but maybe on some future occasion we could go a bit more up-market?'

'I'm always available if there's food involved,' Lizzie joked, then added, 'Don't worry, I won't hold you to your offer.'

'How are you fixed for next Thursday?' was Todd's surprising reply.

Lizzie's eyes widened in dismay. 'You're not serious?'

'Hardly the reaction I was looking

for,' Todd grumbled with a good-natured smile.

'You don't have to. I mean, I thought you were being polite.'

'There's an Oriental-themed evening at The Cove Brasserie down on the seafront. A friend of mine is arranging it and I half promised him I'd put in an appearance. Do you like Chinese food?'

'It's my favourite.' The words were out before Lizzie had time to think.

'Great. You can talk me through the dishes. I don't know a prawn ball from a deep fried mushroom and if you can help me with the chopsticks, I'll be for ever in your debt. I've never been able to master the things.'

Lizzie wasn't sure how to cope with a Todd who wasn't busy accusing her of being involved with his brother or intent on getting her hands on family assets.

'Thursday it is,' she agreed with a shaky smile.

'Now do you have everything you need here?' Todd asked, unaware of the thoughts going through Lizzie's head.

He shrugged on his leather jacket and picked up his car keys. 'You've got my mobile number, haven't you? If there's a problem give me a call.'

Waving him off, Lizzie powered up the computer and settled down in front of the screen.

The security officer poked his head round the door once to check on her and once to deliver the pizza that the driver had left at the main gate.

'Makes a change to have a bit of company of an evening,' he said, joining her for a mug of coffee. 'It can get lonely at times.'

'Would it be all right if I worked on some of my own things later?' Lizzie asked as she came to the end of Todd's work. 'I've got a rush job,' Lizzie explained, 'and I'd like to stay on for a bit longer.'

'So long as you don't let on to the others,' the guard replied.

The telephone rang as Lizzie was signing out of the computer program.

'How's it going?' Todd asked.

'I've just finished and the pizza was lovely, thank you.'

'My pleasure. Don't forget to leave the key with security. We're not at risk from intruders, but you never know. See you tomorrow.'

A buzzing from Lizzie's handbag indicated a call on her mobile.

'Lizzie? It's Charlie. No worries, but . . . '

'What is it?' Lizzie demanded.

'I could have got it wrong,' she began, 'but I'm sure I'm right.'

'What are you talking about, Charlie?'

'I was drawing the curtains in my room,' Charlie began again, 'and as I looked out the window that man with the creepy eyes was parked outside. I first saw him an hour ago and he's still there.'

Stories From The Past

The Cove Brasserie was tucked away in a sandy bay surrounded by a dramatic backdrop of angular cliffs. Access was down wide steps carved in the rock face.

'I'll go first,' Todd volunteered. 'The surface is worn and uneven in places. Hang on to the rope railing and you shouldn't lose your balance.'

'Are you sure these steps are safe?' Lizzie tucked a springy curl of hair back under her hat. Experience had taught her that a seafront brasserie could be a draughty place and she had dressed for comfort rather than fashion.

'Course they are, but most people opt for the small lift that goes up and down the cliff face.'

'There's a lift?'

'Yes.'

'Now he tells me.' Lizzie bit down a

gasp of exasperation. 'I was wondering why we appear to be the only adventurous spirits foolhardy enough to attempt a spot of evening mountaineering.'

Five minutes later, puffed from their exertions, Todd and Lizzie gained firm ground.

'Made it, how are the legs?' Todd looked down at Lizzie's black tights and stout boots. 'You've done this sort of thing before, haven't you?'

'Why do you think I'm dressed like this?' Lizzie extended wax jacket-clad arms. 'And thanks for asking. My legs are fine but like their owner they may have a grumble in the morning.'

'You're coming adrift.'

'What?' Lizzie asked in alarm, hoping her arm gestures hadn't revealed too much flesh.

Todd moved towards her and tucked a frayed end of scarf back into the neck of her jacket. He was close enough for her to feel his breath on her cheek.

'There, is that better?'

'Thank you.' Lizzie cleared the obstruction in her throat, trying to convince herself it was the sea air affecting her vocal chords and not Todd's masculine charisma.

He took a backwards step. The fairy lights guiding the path of the steps softened the harsh angles of his face. Lizzie was glad she could blame the climb down the cliffs for her heightened colour as another warm wash of heat began to work its way up her neck.

'If you've recovered, we'll get going.' Todd was speaking again.

'We won't have to go back the same way, will we?' Lizzie cast a glance up the steep cliff face.

'I didn't think you were a coward?' Todd teased.

'There are only so many stone steps a girl can take in one day.'

'In that case we'll use the lift. The cabin faces out across the harbour and it looks very pretty when it's lit up.'

The brisk evening breeze was doing nothing to fan the flames of Lizzie's glowing complexion. She began to wish Todd would start accusing her of pursuing Steve for his inheritance — that way she would have a reason for feeling flushed. As it was, it seemed he was going out of his way to be pleasant to her.

'Hungry?'

Lizzie nodded. Lunch had been half a gulped down sandwich and a couple of mouthfuls of tea in between working on Jessie's curtains.

'In that case, let's get going again.' Todd linked his fingers through Lizzie's. 'You don't mind, do you?' He squeezed the palm of his hand against hers. 'Only you need to watch your footing. It can get a bit damp along here of an evening.'

His fingers felt rough and warm against hers. Lizzie did her best to give a casual smile of agreement.

'Don't forget your promise.' Todd's voice nudged her attention back.

Lizzie frowned. 'Sorry?' she asked, not getting his drift.

'To translate the dishes?' he prompted. 'Wouldn't want to find I'm tucking into a plate of seaweed.'

Not looking where she was going as she listened to Todd, Lizzie lost her footing when a jutting piece of cliff snagged at her tights.

'Steady.' Todd put his arms round her.

'Where exactly are we?' she demanded, her body stiffening against his.

'We are standing on one of the most beautiful parts of the coastline.'

Todd's voice was a warm murmur in her ear. 'Can't you hear it?'

'Hear what?'

'Nature's nightlife, it's all around you.'

Right now all Lizzie could hear was a buzzing in her ears that had nothing to do with the local nightlife, natural or otherwise.

'Nature in all its beauty. Look at the sculptured cliffs and the shoreline.'

Obediently she raised her eyes up to the stark silhouettes etched against the twilight sky. Mark had been keen on sailing but his crowd preferred the social side of sea life. This was sea life in all its raw beauty.

'It is something else, isn't it?' Lizzie gazed in awe at the ragged outline overshadowing them. Somewhere in the distance she heard the faint mew of a gull as it settled down for the night.

A smile tugged the corners of Todd's mouth. 'Wait 'til you see the dinosaurs.'

'You can remember back that far? I am impressed.'

'Laugh at your peril. They don't take prisoners in this part of the world.'

'Thanks for the warning.' Lizzie was still looking up at the craggy peaks dominating the skyline. 'I can look after myself.'

'As you keep reminding me,' Todd murmured in her ear, 'but we all need a bit of protection sometimes.'

There was no longer a lighthearted look in Todd's eyes. Lizzie cleared her throat.

'Hadn't we better get moving before

they run out of food?' she asked in an attempt to defuse the tension.

She blinked moisture from the sea off her eyelashes and hoped Todd wouldn't think she was getting emotional. He was close enough to her for Lizzie to feel the dark stubble on his chin.

'Of course, I'd forgotten your healthy appetite.' Todd unlinked his fingers from hers. The gesture made his hands feel cold. Her body felt colder, too, without the protection of his presence by her side. 'It's around the next bend.'

Lizzie did her best to pace her steps to his long strides. As they turned the corner, she caught sight of coloured lights reflected in the water. A gust of wind rippled the reflection turning it into a huge kaleidoscope of painted beads.

'Beautiful, isn't it?' Todd murmured in her ear, lowering his voice as if not to disturb the magic of the moment.

'Breathtaking,' Lizzie agreed.

A rush of voices and the sound of loud laughter from the brasserie broke the spell. They drew apart.

'The Peking Duck awaits,' Todd announced as he pushed open the door.

'Is it always like this?' Lizzie raised her voice in order to be heard above the noise.

'It'll probably be quite a crush, too,' Todd warned. 'Nick doesn't do things by halves. He's a man who knows everyone and he invites them all to his parties.'

Colourful Chinese lanterns dangled outside the Oriental teahouse. Two huge statues of fire-breathing dragons guarded the doors and colourful Mandarin paintings decorated the lobby. In the corner of the reception area a water feature trickled through a Chinese pagoda and two lovers clung to each other on a small bridge spanning a fast flowing stream.

'Would you look at that?' Lizzie pointed to the display. 'It's exactly like the famous willow pattern, you know the one you always see on tea plates?'

'The one about unrequited love?' Todd handed their coats to a kimono-clad attendant.

Lizzie turned back to him in surprise. He was the first man of her acquaintance who knew what she was talking about.

'I had an art teacher who was into Oriental culture,' he explained, 'now come on.'

The fragrant cooking smells wafting through from the restaurant area made Lizzie's mouth water.

'Todd. Hi, there!' A voice boomed at them from behind the water feature. A red-faced man emerged from the darkness and beamed at Todd as the two men greeted each other.

'Good to see you.' Nick shook Todd's hand.

'Lizzie Hilton,' Todd introduced them. 'Nick Jackson.'

'Glad to meet you.'

Nick subjected Lizzie to a bone-crushing handshake and smiled at her with practised ease.

He moved away to greet yet more newcomers.

'Let's find a table and tuck in.' Todd

nudged Lizzie forward. 'I'm starving. By the way, thanks for all the work you did on those spreadsheets. They were a great help. Come on. Use your elbows if you think you're going to get crushed. This is no time to be polite. It's every man for himself.'

Todd guided her through the melee of guests heading towards the buffet that had been laid out on trestle tables on the decking.

'Your drinks are on the table,' Nick called over from behind the bar. 'I've managed to snaffle you a couple of seats but don't take too long about it or someone else might lay claim to them. Nice guys come last here.'

Lizzie urged him on, adding, 'The queue's building up behind you.'

'What? Sorry,' Todd looked over his shoulder. 'You'd better go in front of me,' he said with a smile to the female standing behind him.

'Lizzie? It is you, isn't it?'

A girl she remembered vaguely from her sailing days with Mark greeted her.

141

Lizzie's heart sank. She should have realised there might be some faces here she would recognise.

'Er, hello,' Lizzie tried to remember her name.

'Virginia,' the girl added before casting an enquiring look at Todd. 'Are you part of the sailing set?'

'Fraid not,' Todd replied,

'So what's your connection with Lizzie?'

'I suppose you could say I'm her landlord.'

'Indeed? Well I'm glad she's fallen on her feet,' Virginia's arch smile did not reach her eyes. 'We were worried about her after all that unpleasant business. None of us believed those nasty stories of course, but mud does stick, doesn't it?' She placed a manicured hand on Todd's arm. 'Silly me.' She tapped the sleeve of his polo shirt. 'Of course I recognise you now. It's Todd Baxter, isn't it?'

'Have we met?' he asked with a puzzled frown.

'I know your brother, Steve. Give him my regards when you next see him, won't you?' She turned her attention back to Lizzie. 'We must catch up again some time. I'm dying to hear all that you've been up to. I understand you've set up in business on your own. Clever girl. You must be doing well if you can afford to rent one of Baxter's units, unless of course you've structured a special deal? Well done,' she added in a stage whisper that was loud enough for Todd to overhear. 'I admire the way you picked yourself up and started over, really I do.'

'Friend of yours?' Todd queried.

Virginia had already moved down the queue and pounced on her next victim.

'Not exactly,' Lizzie replied, her earlier appetite deserting her.

'Glad to hear it. I hope Steve isn't entangled with her.'

Todd re-addressed his attention to the buffet.

'Is that all you're having?' he asked, glancing at the two prawns and slice of mushroom on Lizzie's plate.

'It's very warm and I, er, don't think I feel like eating much.'

'Nonsense.' Todd dismissed her excuses with a wave of the serving spoon he was clutching. 'Here, have some of this chicken.' He sniffed as he served her a crispy fried wing. 'Think it's been coated in sweet and sour sauce. Egg noodles?' Before Lizzie could object, Todd piled some on her plate.

Todd finished loading their plates. 'Now cutlery. At the risk of further upsetting Nick, let's go for traditional knives, forks and spoons, shall we? Chopsticks might prove too much of a temptation.'

'To do what?' Lizzie asked.

'Dig them into your friend, Virginia, for a start.'

'I don't know her that well really.'

'Strikes me she's the sort of person who likes to poke her nose into everyone else's business. Poor old Steve might have met his match there. This our table?'

The next few moments were spent sorting out their drinks and chairs.

'I never was any good at balancing a plate and a glass and trying to make polite conversation to people I don't really know. Now tuck in.'

The raised voices around them made conversation difficult and for a few moments Todd and Lizzie ate in silence.

'Told you you were hungry,' Todd said as Lizzie finished her last prawn.

'It must have been the amateur rock climbing,' Lizzie agreed as she pushed her empty plate away.

'On the house.' Nick deposited two more drinks on their table. 'Did you enjoy your meal?'

'Very much. Thank you.' Lizzie smiled up at him, doing her best to stifle a yawn.

'You've been working her too hard,' Nick berated Todd. 'Who would want to be *his* secretary,' he confided to Lizzie.

'Lizzie's not my secretary,' Todd corrected him.

'Don't tell me the pair of you are romantically involved?' Nick rolled his eyes. 'Wonders will never cease. I thought you'd never settle down, Todd. Always too worried about Steve making the wrong decision to bother with your own life, weren't you?'

'We're not romantically involved, either,' Lizzie put in swiftly.

'Coming.' Nick signalled to a friend across the room. He winked at Lizzie. 'See you.'

'Sorry about that.' A rueful smile curved Todd's lips. 'When it comes to tittle tattle, Nick can be as bad as your friend, Virginia.'

Lizzie sagged against the back of her chair. The heat from the buffet and the crush of bodies coupled with a recent lack of sleep were making her feel tired.

She blinked her eyes in an attempt to stifle another yawn.

'You haven't been overdoing things, have you?' Todd demanded.

'Sort of,' Lizzie admitted. 'I've got a rush job on for Jessie Price.'

'That actress friend of Olivia's, married to Danny Winter?'

'Do you know her?'

'I knew her step-niece, Stephanie,' Todd replied after a pause.

Too late. Lizzie remembered what Jessie had told her about Todd and Stephanie and how Todd had broken her heart.

'I, um, is it OK to talk about Jessie?' Lizzie asked, hoping she wasn't raking up past injustices.

'Fine by me,' Todd replied, seemingly unruffled.

'Jessie is throwing a birthday party for Danny and she wants new curtains.'

'Who's going to notice the curtains at a party?' Todd asked, a look of male incredulity on his face.

'She's worried the old ones will look shabby.'

Todd leaned forward, his brown eyes searching Lizzie's face. 'There are dark circles under your eyes.'

'I have been burning the midnight oil,' she admitted.

'Words to the wise, whatever she says to the contrary Jessie Price is loaded so charge her accordingly.'

'She paid me a premium to get the job done on schedule.'

Lizzie hoped Todd wouldn't start asking awkward questions. She'd taken to working over at Maiden Farm ever since Charlie had seen Paul parked outside her flat. She wasn't actually breaking the terms of her lease, but she suspected her schedule stretched them to their limits.

'Well, tonight you are having a well-deserved night off.' Todd leaned back in his chair.

Aware of the speculative glances being thrown their way by various females hanging around their table, Lizzie began to wonder how she could have thought Steve was the more handsome of the two brothers.

Todd possessed an air of masculinity that Steve could never hope to attain. Steve was charming, but it was something he didn't have to work at.

Todd, Lizzie imagined, had to work hard at everything he did and that work ethic was reflected in the caring way he was looking at her now. Todd knew what it was like to struggle.

'Have you always lived with Olivia?' Lizzie asked, wanting to know more about him.

'Ever since our parents died. Steve and I were almost too young to remember them and although Monty and Olivia never tried to take their place in our hearts, they were brilliant grandparents. Steve and I used to get up to all sorts of scrapes. We used to pull the wool over poor old Monty's eyes something rotten. I think Olivia suspected what we were up to but she always turned a blind eye.' Todd frowned. 'That's why I don't like to see her upset now.'

'You mean Steve?'

'It's time he settled down.'

'I agree, but you've got to stop playing the big brother.'

'You sound as though you speak from

experience.' Todd looked at her with raised eyebrows.

'Let's say I know what it's like. Besides weren't you always advising Steve to wait until the right female came along in case he made the wrong decision and chose a female who was only after his inheritance?' Lizzie asked.

'You're not going to let me forget that, are you?' Todd made a wry face.

'That was unfair of me,' Lizzie acknowledged.

'I got it wrong and I'm sorry, although you've got to admit it was a natural assumption to make. I mean you were alone in Steve's cottage at night surrounded by bags. It looked as though you were about to move in and Olivia was convinced Steve was involved with a female.'

Before Lizzie could respond a shadow crossed their table.

'I must say I was surprised when Virginia said you were here. I thought you worked late every night, or were you avoiding my company?' Paul looked across the table. 'Paul Owen,' he introduced himself. 'And you must be Todd Baxter.'

An Emergency

Todd slid a newspaper cutting across the table towards her. Lizzie felt the colour drain from her face. She realised how foolish she had been not to take her mother's advice to get the newspaper to publish a retraction, but it was too late to put the record straight now. She had retained her dignity by keeping quiet, although it would seem at the cost of her personal integrity.

'It doesn't make good reading, does it?' The expression on Todd's face was giving nothing away.

'Paul gave it to you last night?'

It was a pointless question but Lizzie felt duty bound to ask it.

'When you left so suddenly last night he said it was probably because of your past history. When I asked him what he meant by that remark he e-mailed me a copy of his local newspaper.

'And you believe this story?'

'What was I supposed to think? You didn't hang around to put your side of things.'

'None of it's true,' Lizzie insisted.

Todd seemed a completely different person from her companion of the previous evening.

'Then give me a good reason to believe you.'

'Because I don't tell lies.'

Todd had called her into his office first thing the morning after their night out at the brasserie. The sick feeling in the pit of Lizzie's stomach trebled when she had seen the print out on his desk.

'I've never lied to you,' she insisted.

'What about Steve?'

'What about him?'

'He's planning on getting married.'

Lizzie gulped down a blockage in her throat. She wasn't sure how they had got on to the subject of Steve's marriage but it looked like another minefield was about to explode.

'Are you now going to tell me you

didn't know anything about it? Or that you hadn't heard from him when you knew how concerned I was?'

'I didn't like pretending to you, Todd but I didn't lie to you.' Lizzie paused.

'I shall do everything in my power to stop the marriage going ahead.'

'You can't.' Lizzie was outraged. 'Steve is a grown man and last night you were saying you wanted him to settle down.'

'He's too irresponsible. Why else would he get involved with someone who has a track record like yours?'

'What? No,' Lizzie protested as she realised Todd was still under the impression she was romantically involved with Steve. 'You don't understand.'

'Then enlighten me.'

'You must believe me, Todd, I have never told you an untruth.' Lizzie knew she was repeating herself but the scenario she faced was worse than she could have imagined.

'Not even when you promised not to work late at your unit? Don't bother to deny it. I've spoken to the security guard involved.'

'I did it because Paul Owen was stalking me and I made sure I didn't infringe the rules.'

'Then why didn't you come to me direct and ask for help?'

'Because I was afraid Paul would do something like this.' Lizzie snatched at the newspaper. 'I had hoped things would blow over and he would get tired of waiting outside my flat. I had Jessie's curtains to complete so I worked on but never past ten o'clock at night.'

'You tell a credible story, I'll give you that.'

'It's not a story. It's the truth.'

'Then why did you run out on me last night?'

'It was a stupid thing to do, but I wasn't thinking straight.'

'It was more than stupid, I'd say it was the action of someone who had a guilty secret to hide.'

Lizzie had left early while Todd was talking to Paul. Knowing she would be no match for Paul and his accusations, she left a message with one of the waiting staff to tell Todd she had developed a headache and that she was going home.

A cable car had been about to leave and she had jumped into it. It was only as it was making its progress up the cliff face that she realised how foolish she had been by running away.

Lizzie took a deep breath. She longed to tell Todd the truth about her broken engagement but that would mean involving other innocent people in her story and she had no wish to go over old ground. Mark was happily married and getting on with his life away from the influence of his brother, Paul.

It was better to accept the inevitable, Lizzie decided, before things turned really nasty. Todd would in time find out about Pearl and Steve but she hoped by then the pair of them would be safely married. Like Mark, Steve needed to get away from his older brother's influence.

'I now find it's been one story after another with you,' Todd said. 'I don't know what to believe any more and that's a situation I cannot tolerate.'

'Are you giving me notice to vacate my unit?'

'I am.'

'Am I allowed to stay on until I've finished Jessie's curtains? The machine is all set up and I've laid everything out and done all the measurements.'

'I want you out of here by the end of the day.'

'You can't do that. I signed a lease.'

'And you've broken the rules of your tenancy. What's worse is that you've involved another member of staff in your plans.'

'I didn't mean to get the security guard into trouble.' Lizzie now felt sick with guilt.

'You're lucky you didn't. He's a reliable, honest employee and in view of his employment history we're not taking the matter further.'

'Todd?' One of the drivers poked his

head round the door. 'Sorry to interrupt but we should be leaving soon if you want to miss the traffic.'

'I'll be with you in a minute.'

Todd gathered up his papers.

'By the way I would prefer it if you didn't go running to Olivia with your tale of woe. You've caused enough disruption in this family.'

The wind caught the door of his office as he strode out and the draught slammed it shut behind him, sending Paul's press cutting cascading to the floor. A hot lump of anger lodged at the back of Lizzie's throat. Moving carefully she stooped down and picked up the paper and placed it under a glass paperweight. No doubt Todd would want to keep it for his records, to remind him of his family's narrow escape from the clutches of a female gold digger.

She watched his car drive out of the compound.

Lizzie decided she would take a holiday after she had completed Jessie's curtains. It had been ages since she had met up with her sister. Florence would be pleased to see her and would probably volunteer Lizzie into digging muddy foundations for her latest project, exactly the right thing she needed to relieve her angst.

A light flashed on Todd's telephone indicating an incoming call on his personal line. Lizzie ignored it.

'Todd?' A voice croaked down the line. 'Are you there? If you are pick up the receiver.'

After a moment's indecision Lizzie flicked back the switch.

'Olivia? What's wrong?'

'I've fallen down the . . . '

The line went dead.

* * *

'Olivia?' Lizzie hammered on the back door of Maiden Farm. The stout wood stung the palm of her hand. 'Open up,' she bellowed.

Not wanting to further involve

security in her actions for what could prove to be a wild goose chase, Lizzie had jumped in her van and hurtled up to the main house.

She could hear the dog barking madly as she tried to gain access to the house. Moments later it appeared at the French window. His paws scratched the glass as he tried to get out.

'Good boy. Stand back,' Lizzie instructed then grabbing up a brick she smashed at the glass. It shattered in one blow. She put a hand through the jagged edge and managed to unlock the door.

'Where are you?' Lizzie collided with the over-excited dog as he hit her with his tail.

She found Olivia at the foot of the stairs, her leg twisted underneath her body. Her face was pale with pain.

'Can you move?' Lizzie asked.

'Not sure,' Olivia moaned. 'I stumbled on the stairs. Stupid ghost pushed me, I think. Must be ma-in-law getting her revenge.' Olivia's feeble attempt at a joke caused her to wince in more pain. 'Today would have been her birthday. Sorry, I'm rambling.'

'I've got to summon help, Olivia.'

'Don't leave me,' she implored. 'I think I might be able to get up if you give me an arm to lean on.'

'No. Stay where you are,' Lizzie ordered her. 'It's important you don't move.'

Olivia's nails dug into the flesh of Lizzie's arms as she clung to her for support.

'My fingers aren't as nimble as they used to be. The dog jumped up at me as I was making my call and I dropped my mobile. It's under that chest I think. Can you get it for me? It was a present from the boys. I don't want to lose it. It's my lifeline.'

'I'll get it as long as you lie still and don't move.'

'That's all I've been doing for the past hour.'

'Found it.' Lizzie emerged from

under the oak chest, her shirt covered in dust. Quickly she punched in the emergency number. Her call was answered on the second ring. 'We need an ambulance.'

'You promised not to leave me.' Olivia clutched on to her arm again as she finished her call.

'I won't, and the emergency services will be here as soon as they can,' Lizzie assured her. 'Can you remember what happened?'

'It was our bridge evening last night. I overslept because I didn't get to bed until late,' Olivia explained through another spasm of pain. 'I would have asked Todd to come and collect me but you were out at that Chinese evening, weren't you? How did it go? Did you have a nice time?'

'Don't try to talk.' Lizzie turned away from the enquiring look in Olivia's eyes.

She struggled to sit upright. 'I'm cold,' she complained.

Lizzie whipped a shrug off one of the

chairs and gently covered Olivia's exposed legs.

'There, is that better?'

'You're a good girl,' Olivia said with a tired smile. 'Why Steve didn't run off with you, I don't know. Now how did you get on with that other grandson of mine last night?'

'We'll talk about it later, Olivia,' Lizzie stalled her. 'The ambulance men will want to know all the details of your fall.'

'Fell over my dressing-gown cord on my way down to let the dogs out,' Olivia admitted.

'Your ankle's very swollen.'

'It gave an almighty crack as I landed. Have you had words with Todd?' Olivia peered at Lizzie in the darkness of the hall. 'I warned you he could be tricky.'

A blue light reflected on the polished wood of the banisters.

'The ambulance is here. I'll let them in.' Lizzie stood up, relieved not to have to answer Olivia's questions. 'Is the front door unlocked?'

'The keys are in my handbag.' Olivia gestured towards the kitchen. 'You will come with me, won't you?'

'I ought to contact Todd.'

'He's out all day. Tell him tonight, when he's back. I can't be doing with him upsetting the nursing staff.'

'What about the dogs?'

'Leave a note for the cleaning lady. She'll be here shortly.'

With swift efficiency the ambulance men strapped Olivia on to a stretcher while Lizzie scribbled a note and left it on the kitchen table.

'My grandson's fiancee is coming with me,' Olivia announced to one of the ambulance men.

'Olivia,' Lizzie hissed as they were loaded into the ambulance, 'I am not engaged to either of your grandsons.'

'My leg.' Olivia ignored her and raised a theatrical hand to her brow.

'Sorry, madam, if you could get your grandson's fiancée,' the ambulance man winked at Lizzie, 'to move over, we can all sort ourselves out.'

The journey to the local hospital took half an hour, during which time Olivia managed to elicit significant details of the driver's personal life, together with that of his second in command.

'I'd like to keep Mrs Baxter in overnight,' the consultant advised Lizzie after he called her into his office. He looked down at his notes. 'Her grandsons are both away?'

'Yes, but what about her ankle?'

Lizzie had been waiting for over three hours in the sterile reception area. Her back was stiff from sitting on an uncomfortable plastic chair and her nerves were at breaking point. She hadn't dared leave the waiting area, for fear of being called in her absence.

'It's badly sprained but no bones broken. She had a good fall if there is such a thing, but in view of her age and possible concussion we would like to keep an eye on her overnight. I don't want her going back to an empty house.'

'Can I stay with her?' Lizzie asked.

'For a little while if you want to, but I don't think you'll get much out of the lady. We've given her something to make her drowsy. You look as though you could do with a pick-me-up as well. Why don't you go and get a cup of tea in the snack bar and something to eat while we arrange a bed for her?'

The tea was hot and strong and revived Lizzie's flagging senses. She nibbled on a chocolate biscuit. Although she hadn't eaten anything all day she wasn't hungry. She checked her mobile. There were several missed messages but mindful of the hospital's policy on making telephone calls on its premises, she didn't return any of the calls.

'I was wondering what had happened to you.' Olivia greeted Lizzie with a sleepy smile as she made her way down the ward.

'I've been having a cup of tea.' Lizzie sat down by her bed. She drew the curtains to afford them some privacy.

'Is there anything you need?'

'Nothing, everyone's been so kind and you have been an absolute angel. I'm sorry to have caused such a fuss,' Olivia apologised.

'You're forgiven as long as you don't do it again,' Lizzie chided her. 'It was a lucky thing I was in Todd's office and heard your call.'

'What were you doing there?' Olivia's eyelids were beginning to droop. 'You never did tell me about your night out.'

Moments later a gentle snoring from the bed told her Olivia had followed her instructions.

'I'm afraid I'm going to have to ask you to leave.' One of the nursing staff drew back the curtains. 'If you like you can phone in the morning to see how your grandmother is.'

'I'm not her granddaughter,' Lizzie began to explain.

'Aren't you? I'm sure I put you down as next of kin. As long as we have a contact number for her that should be sufficient.'

Although the day had been warm, it was cool outside and Lizzie shivered in her short-sleeved shirt.

Swiftly dialling the number of a taxicab she tried to get her thoughts in order. Todd would need to know what had happened. Steve, too.

'Can you drop me here?' she asked the driver as he approached Maiden Farm.

'The industrial unit is closed this time of night,' he advised her.

With a sinking heart Lizzie realised she was too late to clear out her unit. She hoped Todd wouldn't take it into his head to impound her belongings.

'Can you take me up to the farmhouse?'

The driver did a ninety-degree turn and headed down the main drive.

'Some people should learn how to park.' He chuckled as he performed a neat manoeuvre around Lizzie's hastily abandoned van. 'Looks like you've got visitors,' he added as she counted out her change for the fare, adding a tip for all his trouble. 'See you,' he reversed and drove off.

A shadowy figure was lurking by the entrance to the farmhouse.

'Todd?' Lizzie peered into the darkness. 'Is that you?'

'No, he's not here,' came the reply.

She heard movement on the gravel and realised two people, not one, were approaching.

'Where is everybody? Olivia's not answering her door.'

'Steve?' she recognised his voice.

'Lizzie, good to see you. Let me introduce you.' He steadied himself on his crutches. 'Lizzie Hilton, meet Pearl Baxter, my wife.'

New Plans

'Lizzie and I have already met.' Pearl appeared at his side, pretty in a pale pink dress and matching bolero jacket. She was clutching a large hat and looked the picture of happiness.

'I know.' Steve kissed her. 'But I like referring to you as my wife.'

'You're married?' All other thoughts temporarily fled from Lizzie's mind.

Pearl waggled her left hand at Lizzie. On the third finger a white gold diamond ring sparkled back at her.

'Congratulations.'

'I haven't told my father yet,' Pearl confessed. 'We thought we'd get the Baxter side of things sorted first. We were hoping Todd would be here.' She looked round anxiously. 'He seems to have gone walkabout.'

'We can't find Olivia either,' Steve said.

'She's had a fall,' Lizzie said.

Pearl gave a small shriek. 'Olivia's had an accident?'

'Yes.'

'Where is my grandmother?' Steve demanded.

'In hospital. She took a tumble down the stairs and she's twisted her ankle rather badly. I found her,' Lizzie explained.

'When was this?'

'Earlier today. There was no-one else around so I called the emergency services. I've just got back from the hospital.'

'Where's Todd?'

'He's away on a business trip and Olivia didn't want me to call him back so he doesn't know what's happened.' Lizzie sagged against Steve as her voice gave out. 'You should have been here.'

'Well, now I am here I'm taking charge,' he announced firmly. 'Let's all go inside. Pearl can you sort out some coffee? Lizzie looks dead on her feet.'

'So there you have it,' Lizzie forked up the last of the surprisingly good omelette Pearl had rustled up in the kitchen and insisted she eat. 'Thank you, that was delicious, Pearl,' she added.

'Isn't she a dream? Thanks, darling.' Steve passed her their cleared plates and poured out more coffee. 'Not a very good start to married life for you, is it? And I promised you a honeymoon in the Caribbean.'

'There's plenty of time for that.' Pearl blew him a kiss. 'It's good to feel useful. I'll go and stack the dishwasher.'

'And I must get home.' Lizzie stood up. 'Can I leave you to contact Todd, Steve?'

'Er.' Steve hesitated, an uneasy look on his face. 'Right.'

'He is your brother,' Lizzie's patience was now wearing thin with the Baxter men.

'Steady on, Lizzie. No need to rattle my cage.'

'Sorry.'

'It's Todd, isn't it?' Steve's eyes narrowed. 'What's he been doing to upset you?'

Lizzie decided not to go down the route of her recent bust up with Todd. It would only complicate issues and right now Olivia was top of their priority list.

'Everything's fine,' she glossed over his question. 'And again, congratulations to you and Pearl. Does Olivia know you're married?'

'Not yet.'

'Then you must tell her in the morning when you visit,' Lizzie insisted, hoping the older lady wouldn't be too upset at having missed out on her favourite grandson's wedding.

'Why don't you stay over, Lizzie?' Pearl called through from the kitchen. 'There's plenty of room and to be honest,' she confided, 'I'm not looking forward to meeting Steve's brother.'

Lizzie flapped her hands. 'Thanks for the offer but I don't want to outstay my welcome and, once again, congratulations.'

Waving goodbye to Pearl, Lizzie made her way outside. The night air was soft. Usually the onset of summer made her feel upbeat, but tonight it wasn't working its usual magic on her. Her future was a blank unsettled canvas.

Straightening her van from its crooked state, she righted the steering wheel, reversed out of the ditch then drove slowly and carefully down the drive.

★　★　★

'Did I waken you up?' Jessie's voice was light with amusement. 'You are an old sleepy head. It's gone ten.'

Lizzie's eyes felt as though they had been glued together. She struggled to sit up to take Jessie's call.

'I suppose you were out until late last night? The young have no stamina these days.'

'Jessie, sorry, good morning,' Lizzie mumbled. 'Is there a problem?'

'Nothing to worry about at all, it's only a courtesy call to see how things are going. I'm sitting at my desk enjoying the sunshine and catching up on all my paperwork. So what news?'

Lizzie assured the actress that her drapes were nearly finished.

'In that case we should think about a date for hanging them. Do you have your diary with you?'

Lizzie looked round for her personal organiser then remembered she had left it in her unit at Maiden Farm. She snatched up a scrap of paper and a pen.

'Would Friday afternoon suit?' Jessie asked. 'We should have the place to ourselves.'

'Friday it is,' Lizzie agreed, hoping that would give her enough time to complete the last-minute finishing off.

'By the way,' the tone of Jessie's voice altered.

'Yes?' Lizzie's anxiety level rose. Bad news always travelled fast. Would Jessie have found about Paul's press cutting, too?

'I meant what I said about you coming to the party.'

'As a guest?'

'Of course.' Jessie's tinkling laugh allayed Lizzie's fears. 'I wouldn't want you to whip out your sewing machine and tape measure in the middle of the celebrations. You can bring a partner if you like.'

'That's very kind of you.'

'Acceptances are coming in thick and fast, although I should also warn you I might need you on hand to answer any technical questions that may arise.'

'Technical questions?'

'About curtain material, that sort of thing.'

'I'm not sure how technical you can be on the subject of curtain material.'

'Darling, this is the opportunity of a lifetime to showcase your skills. Don't forget to arm yourself with lots of your little cards. I'd better go. We can talk later. Now don't forget Friday.'

No sooner had Lizzie put the telephone down than there was an urgent knocking on her door.

'Charlie?' She stepped back in surprise. 'What are you doing here?'

'You're back.' She looked relieved. 'I've come to say goodbye.'

'Where are you going?'

'We're off to America next week. Dad's got a job in Silicon Valley and we're all going with him.'

'America?'

Lizzie wasn't sure how many more shocks her system could take.

'Gran's had an offer on the shop and the flat.'

Charlie was jumping around with joy on Lizzie's doorstep. 'Isn't it amazing?'

'Wonderful news.' Lizzie did her best to inject some enthusiasm into her voice.

Charlie put a guilty hand over her mouth. 'I wasn't supposed to tell you. You won't let on when Gran breaks the news will you?'

'Of course not.'

'At least that horrid man wasn't here last night or the night before,' she said, her young face alight with happiness. 'I'll call you from America.' Charlie was already running back down the steps.

The telephone rang again as Lizzie closed the door.

'Hello?' She snatched up the receiver with a sigh, wondering when, if ever, she was going to get her life back on an even keel.

'Hi, it's Steve here'.

'Any news on Olivia?'

'That's partly why I'm phoning. The hospital says she can come home. She had a good night.'

'Excellent.'

'Pearl and I are going to fetch her later and bring her back here.'

'Is there anything I can do?'

After a short pause Steve said, 'Todd turned up in the small hours. He'd been delayed on the motorway or something.'

'Oh, yes?'

'After that we didn't get much sleep.'

'I can imagine.'

'Actually he took our news rather well after he'd recovered from the shock of finding out we were married and that Olivia was in hospital and that you hadn't done a runner.'

'Sorry?'

'He found your unit unlocked and half your stuff outside.' Steve paused. 'He's filled me in on what's been happening in my absence. I'm really sorry, Lizzie. At times a mountain goat has got more sense than my big brother. I told him exactly what he could do with his paper clipping.'

'You've seen it?'

'I've never heard or read such a load of nonsense in my life. To be honest, by the time Todd got to the punch line I wasn't listening to him. I was so mad about the way he treated you when all you were doing was trying to help. Pearl had to calm us both down. To cut a long story short I've put him right about the situation between us in no uncertain terms but it wasn't easy. It was as if he didn't want to believe me. Goodness knows why. He doesn't like being in the wrong, I suppose.'

'I'm glad it's all sorted out,' Lizzie replied, hoping Steve would hang up soon. She was in desperate need of a cup of tea to revive her flagging senses.

'Pearl has been an absolute saint. She must think as a family we're half mad, but she's been marvellous about things. By the way you've got an open invitation to visit any time. We are in your debt and Pearl and I want you to know we appreciate everything you've done.'

'Thanks, Steve. I would help Pearl out if I could, but I've just learned my landlady is selling up.'

'You don't have anywhere to live?'

'Not for long.'

'That's great news.'

Lizzie coughed in shock. Steve's comment had hardly been the reaction she was looking for.

'What was that?'

'Pearl and I were only discussing it this morning.'

'Discussing what?'

'What to do with Wrenn Close.'

'You're selling up, too?'

'Far from it. We want to move in but we can't until Olivia's better. I am uneasy about the cottage being empty but you can solve our problem.'

'How?'

'By moving in. With the place unoccupied you can work on colour schemes and stuff and not be interrupted.' Steve's voice was full of excitement. 'You will do it, won't you?'

In a daze Lizzie found herself agreeing to Steve's plan.

'That'll cheer Pearl up. She's dreading today. She's got to tell her father about us. Some tabloid journalist has got hold of the story and apparently they're going to publish it tomorrow.'

Moving On

A note taped to her unit doors informed Lizzie that security had sealed them and accepted no responsibility for any loss or damage suffered as a result of their action.

Lizzie put her hands on her hips as she inspected the clutter inside her workshop. How could she have amassed so much in such a short space of time? Security hadn't been too fussy about placement and Jessie's curtains were now draped over one of Steve's workbenches. Grateful that they had at least treated them with care, she eased past a bolt of velvet, careful not to dislodge any of her sewing supplies.

It would take a while to move everything out, but the most important task, Lizzie decided, was to make sure Jessie's curtains were carefully handled.

She knew she would also at some

time have to go up to the farmhouse to collect the keys to Steve's cottage. There had been no sign of Todd when she had driven in to the compound for which she was grateful. The lights were on his office but she could see through the windows that no one was there. If he was visiting Olivia in hospital, she might be able to get through the day without bumping into him and that suited her fine.

'Need any help?'

Lizzie spun round.

'The guard on the gate tells me you're moving out.'

Paul, who had been standing behind her, took a step backwards, a look of alarm on his face.

'OK.' He raised his hands in a conciliatory gesture. 'I know I'm absolutely the last person you want to see in this world, but I've come to apologise. I'm really sorry. I don't know what came over me. I should never have shown the press cutting to Todd.'

'You're ruined my life twice, so you'll

understand when I say I don't believe you.'

'You've every right to be angry with me, but I want you to know I'll try and make things up with Todd.'

'Please don't bother.'

'Why not?'

'You've done enough damage and Todd has already made his mind up about me and that's why I have been asked to leave.'

'I suppose he believed that story in the newspaper?'

'Everybody else did. Why should he be any exception?'

'Why did you leave the restaurant without a word to anyone?' Paul demanded as if what followed was Lizzie's fault.

'It doesn't matter now.'

'Todd asked how we knew each other and after that everything came tumbling out.'

Lizzie turned away from him. 'Just go, Paul.'

'I can't. I have to put things right,' he

insisted. 'Todd will believe me, I'm sure, when I tell him those stories weren't the absolute truth.'

'There was nothing true in them at all.'

'You were engaged to my brother. That bit was true, and the bit about our family business, that was true as well.'

'Whatever you say won't make any difference with Todd.'

'Why not?'

'I've broken the terms of my lease and invalidated my insurance.'

'What have you done?'

'I worked over because I didn't want to go back to the flat.'

'Because I was parked outside?' A look of despair crossed Paul's face. 'I can't say how sorry I am for getting you into such a mess, Lizzie.'

'Paul if you really want to help me, I would appreciate it if you would leave me alone to get on with my life.'

'Are you sure I can't persuade you to accept my help?'

Before Lizzie realised his intention

Paul grasped her elbow and dragged her towards him.

'Why do you keep pushing me away? I could make life easier for you.'

'What I do with my life is absolutely no business of yours.'

Lizzie's raised voice drew the attention of one of her neighbours.

'Anything wrong?' Jack strolled over, still clutching the monkey wrench he had been using then, taking in the situation, approached Paul. 'I think,' he said, 'you'd better leave.'

'Why should I?' Paul narrowed his eyes at Jack.

'Because you're disturbing the peace and annoying the lady.'

'Are you going to try and make me?' Paul sneered.

'I will if I have to.'

As Jack advanced towards Paul, he slipped on some mud and the next moment his feet went from under him.

'No.' Lizzie intervened in an attempt to avert a tussle between the two men.

'What exactly is going on here?'

A whiplash sharp voice had the effect of stilling Paul's arm, which had been raised in a threatening gesture.

'Sorry, Todd.' Jack recovered himself first. 'Didn't mean to make a scene.'

Lizzie put out a hand and helped him to his feet. 'You didn't hurt yourself, did you?' she asked.

'I'm used to spending half my day on my back, although,' he added, a rueful smile curving his lips, 'usually I'm underneath a car.'

'Then I suggest you get back to your car,' Todd cut in, 'and leave me to deal with this.'

Jack looked as though he was about to object.

'That's OK, Jack,' Lizzie assured him, 'and thanks for everything.'

'You know where I am if you want me,' he said before strolling back to his unit.

'Do you have business with Miss Hilton?' Todd turned his attention to Paul.

'It would seem not,' Paul muttered.

'Then I suggest you move on as well.'

Casting a baleful glance in Lizzie's direction Paul now shuffled off, leaving Lizzie to face Todd on her own.

'If you've come to check on my progress, I'm working as fast as I can.' She narrowed her eyes as she squared up to him. 'Unfortunately my move was delayed for reasons outside my control.'

'You don't intend using that implement on me, I hope?' Todd asked in a slightly softer voice.

'What?' Lizzie was having difficulty quelling her heartbeat.

Todd nodded towards the monkey wrench that Lizzie was clutching.

'It's Jack's,' she said, looking at it in surprise, not sure how it came to be in her possession.

'Was there anything else?' she demanded, wishing Todd wouldn't look at her quite so intently.

'Actually there is.' He paused. 'I've come to say thank you and,' he added, 'to apologise.'

'It's not necessary,' Lizzie began, but

Todd didn't appear to be listening.

'I really don't know what I would do if anything happened to Olivia. I've tried to suggest she has a resident companion but she won't hear of it.' An annoyed look crossed his face. 'At times she drives me mad.'

'If it's any consolation I think she drives everyone a little bit mad at times,' Lizzie half smiled.

'How is Olivia?' she managed to ask.

'A bit bruised and battered but she'll recover. Thank heavens you found her in time.'

'I had to break a window to get in. Sorry about that.'

'It's already been seen to by Steve, and Pearl's swept up all the mess. They've gone to fetch Olivia in the car. They intend telling her their news before they bring her home. Olivia will probably want to organise another party to celebrate their marriage.' Todd cast Lizzie an uneasy look as if sensing what was to come.

'Perhaps now you'll believe me when

I say there is nothing between me and Steve?'

Todd flushed under his outdoor tan.

'Things got a bit garbled, didn't they?'

'Is that an apology?' Lizzie demanded.

'Sort of.' Todd's skin tone deepened.

'Well, it's not very clear.' Lizzie crossed her arms.

'Apologising is not something I do well,' Todd admitted, 'well, where Steve is concerned.' He took a deep breath then said in a rush, 'It wasn't my finest hour accusing you of being a gold digger and getting involved with Steve because of his inheritance and I'm sorry for my past behaviour. Will that do?'

Although Lizzie enjoyed watching him look so uncomfortable there was none of the bossy elder brother about his demeanour now.

'And the newspaper interview Paul showed you? You believed that was true, too, didn't you?'

'Running away wasn't the answer.'

'I realise that now,' Lizzie admitted.

'Faults on both sides, wouldn't you say?' Todd moved in closer.

Aware that Jack was looking across at them, Lizzie took a careful step backwards. Todd's eyes flickered an expression akin to disappointment.

'Well,' Lizzie spoke first, 'thanks for the update on Olivia's progress and for the apology. Now if you'll excuse me, I'm rather busy.'

'Look, can we start again. Please?'

'You mean you want me to carry on typing up your spreadsheets?'

'I'm not talking about spreadsheets.' An angry frown creased Todd's forehead. 'I'm talking about us. You don't need to move out if you don't want to.'

'I've already made alternative arrangements,' Lizzie explained.

'No,' Todd now looked puzzled, 'you can't have.'

For a fleeting second Lizzie felt a pang of sympathy for him. He was a man who was used to being in charge and the situation was slipping away from him. Now Steve was married Todd would no longer have total control over the family finances.

'I'm afraid I have so thanks for the offer, but no thanks.'

'You haven't gone to Paul Owen for help, have you?'

'No, I haven't. Now was there anything else?'

'What about Olivia? You can't leave without saying goodbye to her.'

Lizzie hadn't realised that by cutting herself off from Todd she might lose touch with Olivia and she hadn't expected the knowledge to hurt quite so much.

'She wants to invite you to tea next week. Will you come? Please?'

After a brief hesitation Lizzie nodded. The eager look on Todd's face melted into a smile as she added, 'Tell Olivia I'll give her a call. Now I must get on.'

'I nearly forgot.' Todd drew an envelope out of his pocket. 'Steve left this for you on the hall table. I picked it up on my way out.' He handed it over.

'Thank you,' Lizzie replied.

They looked at each other for a few moments before Todd said, 'I'd better get back to the office then. I've a mountain of paperwork to get through.'

Lizzie watched him stride along the footpath, wondering why she felt so deflated at the thought of not seeing him again. Then, angry with herself for displaying such weakness, she ripped open Steve's envelope. A key fell into the palm of her hand.

Move in whenever you like, Steve had written in his bold handwriting. *I'll try to visit once I'm mobile again and I'll make sure no-one knows where you are. You have my promise.*

The note was finished off with a row of kisses.

Lizzie began to fold Jessie's curtains and stow them in the back of her van. There would be plenty of room to finish them off undisturbed in Steve's cottage and that was exactly what she needed right now, a period of peace and quiet.

A Seaside Stroll

Olivia sported a colourful striped patch over her left eye. She beamed at Lizzie from her recumbent position on the sofa.

'Come in, darling. Do you like it? They offered me one of those dreadful black things. I told them if they thought I was wearing something that made me look like Captain Dreadful then they had another thing coming. I'd rather go around sporting a bruised eye for all to see, even if my appearance did frighten the horses.' She guffawed. 'Then Pearl the sweet child went out and managed to get me this one from a toy shop. What do you think?'

Lizzie inspected the rainbow eye-shade.

'Very becoming, Olivia.'

Olivia held out her arms. 'Now come and give me a kiss and tell me how life's been treating you. I'm very cross with you. Fancy thinking you could just walk out of my life without a word of goodbye.'

Lizzie was enveloped in a bear hug.

'Am I forgiven?' Lizzie asked as Olivia finally released her hold.

'Of course you are and never mind all that now. I have missed you,' Olivia said. 'Pearl's a terrific girl, but she's newly married and totally tied up with Steve. She's also a bit ladylike for me. Then there's that father of hers.' Olivia made a face. 'Have you met him?'

'I don't move in racing circles.'

'Just as well.' Olivia shuddered. 'He's trying to organise their lives and they've only been married a short time. I told him not to interfere. Then the wretch tried to say that my Steve wasn't good enough for his daughter. I wasn't having any of that, I can tell you. I told him Pearl was extremely lucky to have Steve as a husband.'

Lizzie settled down in a squashy armchair glad to see Olivia was her normal robust self.

'I can't blame them for going off and getting married on the quiet. I would have liked to have done the same thing with my Monty but his mother wanted the traditional bit and I thought I'd better fall in with her plans. Anyway, where was I?'

'You were telling me about Pearl and Steve's wedding?'

'That's right. They had two witnesses. The man who pushed Steve's wheelchair and a casual visitor and that was it, very sensible of them. There was no chance of Todd or me interfering. The only fly in the ointment was the casual visitor. Unfortunately he recognised Pearl and when he got home he sold his story to one of the tabloids. What a toe rag. If I catch up with him I'll bend his ears back.

'Of course, Pop Mason nearly exploded when he read the exclusive over his breakfast. Pearl didn't manage to tell him in time before it hit the headlines and well, I thought nothing would ever shock me, but he came on the telephone and virtually accused me of having a hand in it. We had a very colourful exchange.' Olivia's face creased up into a happy smile. 'It quite put me back on my feet.'

'Talking of feet.' Lizzie looked down to the footstool to where Olivia was resting her ankle. 'How are yours?'

'Much better, thank you, darling. The swelling has subsided and my left foot is fine but it still hurts like mad if I try to walk on my bad ankle. A nurse comes in once a day and sorts me out and I've got some local help but it'll be a while before I'm completely mobile.'

'I'm pleased to see you're obeying orders.' Lizzie delved into her bag. 'I've brought you some magazines.'

'Would you look at that?' Olivia gasped at the front cover of one of them. A celebrity was gliding down a red carpet waving to her fans.

'I wasn't sure of your tastes so I put in a couple of gardening ones as well.'

'Thank you, darling. I'll look at them later.'

'Can I do anything for you while I'm here?'

'Certainly not. You're a guest. Besides I am being outrageously spoilt. I have two grandsons on the premises and a lovely new granddaughter-in-law.'

It hurt Lizzie to smile. She hadn't realised how much she would miss the Baxter family, infuriating though they were, Todd with his innate belief that his way was right, then Steve for being Steve, and as for Olivia, nearly everything she did infuriated someone.

'What a year we've had,' Olivia reminisced. 'There's Steve still on crutches and me hobbling around on one foot, not to mention elopements and it's still only June. Thank goodness nothing has happened to Todd.'

Lizzie hoped the mention of Todd's name would not bring a flush to her face.

'Anyway, what's been happening to you?' Olivia asked.

'I've been working on Jessie's curtains,' Lizzie began.

'You know perfectly well I'm not talking about curtains. I'm talking about you and Todd, but I dare say you brought it on yourself.'

'Brought what on myself?' Lizzie had been slipping down the cushions in her armchair. Olivia's remark jerked her upright.

'You're too stubborn for your own good at times. You didn't have to move out, you know.'

'I invalidated the insurance on my unit.'

'Piffle.'

'Todd said . . . '

'You should never listen to anything he says if it doesn't suit you. I haven't for years.'

'There was more to it than that.'

'It was that wretched interview, wasn't it?' Olivia demanded. 'I got Steve to print a copy off for me. Talk about fairy tales. Anyone with half a brain could tell the whole thing was made up. A gold digger does not bang around the countryside in a rented van delivering curtains.'

'I've got my own van now,' Lizzie put in. 'The old one gave up the ghost. Jack sorted me out.'

'Newspapers,' Olivia growled. 'They're all grubby. Sorry, darling. I'm only being grumpy because I miss you. Where are you living now?' Olivia's robin brown eyes were alert with suspicion. 'You're not homeless, are you?'

'I'm living in a thoroughly respectable house with four walls and a roof so there's no need to worry.'

'How do I contact you?'

'You've got my mobile number.'

'Why won't you tell me where you are?'

'Because it's only temporary accommodation.'

'That's no reason not to give me your address.'

'Once I get properly settled I'll give you all the details.'

'I promise I won't tell anyone.'

Lizzie knew from experience Olivia could be indiscreet and she didn't want the older woman letting slip her whereabouts. Steve and Pearl were the only two people who knew where she was apart from her mother and for the moment she wanted it to stay that way.

'I suppose that will have to do as long as you promise not to totally disappear out of our lives again.'

'I promise,' Lizzie replied. 'Where are Pearl and Steve?' she asked as Olivia fell silent.

'Pearl's driven Steve to the hospital for a check up.'

'Will they be joining us for tea?'

The sound of something falling off a shelf disturbed them.

'What was that?' Lizzie looked round.

'I didn't hear anything,' Olivia replied, looking deceptively innocent.

'There's someone in the kitchen.'

'Perhaps it's my daily.'

'She let me in on her way out.'

There was more noise from the kitchen and a moment later Todd appeared in the doorway.

'Lizzie? I thought I heard voices. What are you doing here? What's wrong with Olivia?' He frowned at his grandmother.

'There's nothing wrong with me,' Olivia snapped. 'Lizzie's come to tea.'

'Today? You asked me to order a gateau for Friday.'

'No, I didn't.'

'Yes, you did.'

'I think you've got your dates muddled, Todd.'

'No, I haven't.' Todd strode into the room and snatched up the little calendar Olivia used to write down her appointments. 'There, look. It can't have been today. It says here the nurse is due this afternoon to redress your bandage.'

'Does it?' Olivia widened her blue eyes in surprise.

'There's no mention of Lizzie coming to tea.'

'Goodness me.' Olivia did her best but her acting skills had rusted up over the years. 'I must have forgotten about the nurse.'

'In that case,' Lizzie stood up, determined to bring an end to any argument that could be brewing between Todd and his grandmother, 'I'll be going.'

'No.' Olivia grabbed Lizzie's arm with surprising strength. 'Todd, take Lizzie out for tea to make up for your silly error.'

'My silly error?' Todd's voice rose in annoyance.

'It really doesn't matter whose fault it was,' Lizzie insisted. 'Olivia and I can reschedule our tea date for another day.'

'No, we can't,' Olivia objected.

'Why not?' Lizzie and Todd demanded in unison.

'I'm busy. There's a bridge tournament coming up next week.'

'Which you won't be going to.'

'Steve can drive me over if you don't want to.' There was a mulish expression now on Olivia's face.

'With one leg out of action? I don't think so.'

'Then Pearl . . . '

'I expect I could have got my dates muddled.' Lizzie butted in.

'No, you didn't,' Olivia insisted.

'Perhaps it was my fault,' Todd echoed.

'That's what I've been saying all along.' Olivia seized her moment. 'Now Todd, as you don't seem to be very busy this afternoon I suggest you take Lizzie out to tea, and for goodness' sake don't start accusing her of pinching the teaspoons.'

A gamut of emotions crossed Todd's face as he realised Olivia had neatly backed him into a corner.

'Of course,' he agreed, gallantly recovering his composure, 'it will be my pleasure.'

'I don't want to put you to any trouble,' Lizzie replied.

There were times when Olivia went too far and now was one of them. Lizzie wanted to be annoyed with the older woman but her smile was so wickedly complicit that Lizzie's frown faded and she smiled back.

'Where would like to go?' Todd asked.

'That's better.' Olivia nodded approval.

'I'm afraid I'm not dressed to take you anywhere really smart,' he added.

Todd was wearing casual work trousers, an open-necked shirt and a dark jumper that had a hole in the sleeve.

'I did promise you a trip on the cable car?' he suggested.

'A trip on the cable car is a splendid idea,' Olivia put her weight behind him. 'You both spend far too much time cooped up in front of machines. If my memory serves me correctly there's a lovely little tea bar at The Fisherman's Rest. They do the most delicious crab sandwiches and fresh cream pastries in the shape of seashells. Why don't you check them out?'

'Hello, anyone home?' a voice called through from the kitchen.

'Here's my nurse. Lovely girl. She's

Australian. Now off you go the pair of you.'

'I wasn't a party to all that,' Todd attempted to explain as they drove towards the seafront.

'I believe you,' Lizzie replied.

'There's no way Olivia would muddle her dates. She's not half as scatty as she pretends to be. I didn't mention it back there but she called me about an hour ago and asked me to drop by because she was feeling lonely.'

'If you want to cry off I'll understand.' Lizzie felt duty bound to offer.

'Actually.' Todd flicked an indicator switch and turned right onto the coast road. 'I don't.'

Lizzie watched the countryside speed past.

'I've missed you,' he said in a low voice. 'I would have telephoned you.'

'Why didn't you? You had my mobile number.'

'I didn't want to tread on Jack's toes.'

Todd had come across the pair of them huddled under her bonnet in the road outside Maiden Farm a few days after Lizzie had vacated her premises. Lizzie had been busy handing Jack spanners and torque wrenches.

'He was only trying to get my van going again.'

'Then why is it parked outside his cottage every time I drive by?'

'It was on its last legs and the owner sold it to him for spare parts. I used some of Jessie's commission to get myself a new one. Jack helped me there, too. It is his area of expertise,' Lizzie emphasised, wondering why she was taking time out to explain things to Todd.

Another silence descended between them. Lizzie rubbed the tension away from the back of her neck. Over the past week she had managed to move most of her things into Steve's cottage, which was proving to be remarkably cosy.

As she feared, Jessie was proving to be a demanding customer and Lizzie's initial attempt to hang the finished curtains had resulted in a colourful disagreement which had ended in part of the job having to be redone. Lizzie had worked on into the small hours and in the warmth of Todd's car her lack of sleep was getting to her. Her held fell forward and she closed her eyes.

The sound of seagulls circling above them woke her up. The car engine changed note as Todd began his descent down the winding road into the harbour. In the distance the sun bathed the sea a brilliant blue.

'I'm sorry.' Lizzie hid a yawn behind her hand.

'Don't be.' His eyes softened into a smile. 'You've got some colour back in your cheeks and it looks like we've picked a good day for our cable car ride.'

They were the only two passengers on the downward journey and Lizzie moved to the far windows to take in the view.

Todd stood beside her. 'Nick's brasserie.' He pointed across the bay.

'Did we really climb all the way down those steps?' Lizzie looked in amazement at the jutting wedges of stone carved into the cliff face. In the bright sunlight she couldn't believe there were so many.

'There's the old court house and the lifeboat station and the flour mill.' Todd pointed towards the town that was coming into view.

'What's that black thing?' Lizzie squinted into the sunlight

'Nellie? She's our midday gun as the saying goes. She saved the honour of the harbour when we were being attacked way back in The Middle Ages, I think by the French.'

Lizzie was having trouble trying to concentrate. Todd was now standing far too close for comfort.

The little car slid into its moorings slot at the bottom of the cliff with a gentle bump and the doors slid open.

'Fancy a leg stretch along the seafront to work up an appetite before our crab sandwich tea?'

It had been a while since Lizzie had lazed among the dunes watching the world go by and she had missed the sound of the sea and the smell of the day's catch being unloaded. Readily agreeing to Todd's suggestion they set off along the water's edge.

The sun burnished Todd's hair deep chestnut and the lines of tiredness around his eyes creased into another smile as he recalled a childhood outing.

'You know when Steve and I were kids we used to like going down to the beach after a storm to forage around and to see what the sand had thrown up in the way of fossils. You'd be surprised what we found, bits of driftwood, strange shaped seaweed, old fish bones. It was exciting stuff to two young boys.'

'My sister's the same,' Lizzie replied. 'She loved an adventure. It's something she hasn't grown out of and she's never happier than when she's digging around for something.'

Todd slackened his pace. 'It all stopped for Steve and me when our parents died. Steve became scared of the sea and I never came down here again either.'

Todd shaded his eyes from the sun as he looked towards the horizon. 'That's why I worry about him. He used to be so sensitive.'

'He'll be safe with Pearl,' Lizzie said softly. 'Who'll look after you?' Lizzie asked.

'Me?' Todd seemed surprised by the question. 'I looked after myself. Monty and Olivia were marvellous but they were busy people. I just sort of got on with things and didn't bother them. We all rubbed along quite well, really.'

'Is Steve's marriage going to change things between you?'

'I hope not. Pearl's got her head screwed on and she gets on with Olivia, which is a blessing. I think I invented excuses not to like you.' Todd's voice was so low Lizzie had to lean in towards him to hear what he was saying.

'What? Why?'

'I thought you'd come between me

and Steve. Not very grown up behaviour, was it?' Todd admitted with a shamefaced smile. 'I know things can't always stay the same and that Steve and I have reached a turning point in our relationship, but I didn't want to let go. He and Olivia are all the family I have.'

The sun that had temporarily disappeared behind a cloud chose that moment to re-appear.

'I had no intention of coming between you,' Lizzie responded with warmth.

'I didn't know that when I first met you, but I did know you were too independent for Steve. I told you he's artistic, he likes gentle girls.'

Lizzie gave an undignified snort that she managed to disguise as a sneeze. In her opinion Todd had a lot to learn if he thought Pearl was going to be a pushover.

The dying sunlight slanted the harsh planes of Todd's face into softer contours.

'Now we've got all that out of the

way,' he said, 'Olivia did suggest I treat you to a plate of crab sandwiches, so if you've nothing better to do?'

'I have actually.'

'What?' Todd's smile died.

'Come on, I fancy some candy floss, my treat.'

Lizzie laughed at the appalled expression on Todd's face as she dragged him towards the red and white striped kiosk on the promenade. They joined the queue of excited day-trippers.

'Don't complain or I'll force feed you a toffee apple as well.'

'Spare my fillings,' Todd begged as they reached the front of the queue.

'Large of small?' the attendant enquired.

'Two, large,' Lizzie replied as the machine began to spin.

Secrets

'I don't think this is what Olivia meant by taking me out to tea,' Lizzie said in a husky voice as Todd's lips left hers.

'I wouldn't be so sure,' he replied.

After tea they had strolled along the seafront then down into the tiny fishing village, past the white clapboard cottages decorated with colourful hanging baskets. Several had lanterns draped between them, casting colourful shadowy shapes on cobblestones, slippery from where they had been rain-washed by a sudden shower that had sent Todd and Lizzie scurrying for cover in an inn doorway.

A rainbow arced the harbour when they emerged, laughing and breathless and ducking from the drips falling from the hanging baskets.

'The weather's pulling out all the stops.' Todd yanked Lizzie away from a swaying hoarding advertising boat trips around the harbour. 'What say we walk up to the point to get a better view? Walk off all that candy floss?'

Lizzie's legs ached by the time they reached the summit where she discovered to her dismay that the wooden viewing bench was a collapsed heap of broken planks.

'Looks like a victim of a recent storm.' Todd inspected the damage. 'Can you perch on this bit of armrest?'

Lizzie watched Todd try to work the pay telescope as she did her best to balance on the fragile piece of wood.

'I think someone's jammed a coin in the slot,' he complained. 'You'll have to take my word for it that France is that way and,' he turned a ninety degree angle, 'somewhere else is that way.'

'Glad we're not in a boat and relying on your navigational skills to get us back home.' Lizzie rubbed her sore toes.

'I don't think our continental cousins

are planning another invasion this afternoon so they'll be no need for Nellie to re-defend her honour.'

Todd perched beside Lizzie on an adjacent broken piece of wood.

'Ready for the return journey?' he asked after a few moments.

'I am, but I'm not sure about my feet.' Lizzie tried not to wince as she stood up.

'Want me to carry you down?'

Lizzie brushed off Todd's offer, hoping it was a joke.

Two glasses of cider and a fish and chip supper in the harbour were followed by an ascent to the cliff top in the last cable car of the evening. Again they were the only two passengers on board and in the velvet darkness of the car Todd had taken Lizzie in his arms and kissed her.

'You're not going to go all independent on me again are you?' His voice tickled her hair against her ear. 'Because I don't think I'm up to another challenging exchange of views and our relationship has made tremendous strides forwards today, wouldn't you say?'

Lizzie swayed against Todd then rested her head on his chest.

The rough cloth of Todd's work jumper scratched against her fingertips.

'What's that perfume you're wearing?' He sniffed.

'Probably eau de sewing machine oil.'

'That's a new one on me.'

'I had to do a quick bit of tinkering with the tension. Jessie's curtains are quite heavy.'

Todd was now resting his chin against her hair. Lizzie could hear the steady thump of his heartbeat.

'Would you like to come to her party with me?'

Todd jerked back as Lizzie turned to look up at him.

'Steady. Don't want to bang noses,' she complained. 'Jessie's party?' Lizzie prompted when Todd didn't immediately reply. 'She said I could bring a guest.'

Todd circled his arms around her waist as Lizzie turned back to look at the receding harbour beneath them. Colourful lights laced together formed an uneven necklace of blurred reflections in the water. The cable car bumped underneath them as the lights went out.

'Will Stephanie Winter be there?' Todd asked.

The name echoed around the cable car as Lizzie struggled to remember why it was familiar to her.

'We're not moving,' Lizzie replied.

'I hadn't noticed.' Todd nuzzled her hair.

The public address system crackled and the attendant's voice broke into the darkness. 'Journey's end,' he announced.

'Come on, we don't want to get locked in for the night.'

Lizzie stumbled into the yellow light of the booking hall then out into the night air.

Todd's car was the only vehicle in the deserted car park and the attendant had already extinguished the lights.

'Mind the potholes.' Todd came up behind her then muttered a curse as his words were followed by a loud splash, then a squelchy noise. In the darkness it was difficult to see where she was going and Lizzie cannoned into him then yelped as the strap on her summer sandals gave way. Her ankle buckled under her.

'Here, lean on me,' Todd held out his arm. Together they limped towards the car.

'Soon get some heat going.' Todd flicked a switch on the dashboard and Lizzie massaged her ankle back to life.

After a few moments he straightened up.

'That's better.'

As the condensation cleared from the windscreen Lizzie began to remember exactly what it was Jessie had told her about Stephanie Winter. Todd had broken her heart.

'If you must know,' as if reading her mind Todd said, 'Stephanie and I were friends a couple of summers back.'

'It was more serious than that according to Jessie.'

'That's not true,' Todd protested. 'She was at a bit of a loose end for the summer. We went around together for a while but nothing came of it. Then she found herself an American with an oil well and that was that.'

He turned his full attention to the road as they came to a busy stretch of dual carriageway. Lizzie fiddled with the broken strap of her sandals, unable to shake off a feeling of unease.

A fine sea spray misted the windscreen. The wipers swished, creating two clear arcs before more moisture blurred their vision. Lizzie inhaled the smell of wet earth as the tyres splashed over the dampened road surface. Todd slowed up and left the main road and moments later swung the car into the farm driveway.

A shaft of light on the front doorstep widened to reveal a figure standing there.

'Steve?'

Todd opened the car door.

'Hi, there. We were getting worried about you. Olivia said you'd gone out to tea but it's gone ten o'clock. Pearl was about to start searching the net to see if there had been an accident. Where's Lizzie?'

'She's here with me.'

Steve limped through the twilight towards them.

'Don't go, Lizzie. I want a word. Todd, do me a favour and go inside and chat to Pearl for me. There's a good man. I don't want to be overheard.'

'Then I'll leave you to have your private word with Lizzie,' Todd replied. 'If your invitation to attend Jessie's party still holds' he said to Lizzie, 'give me a call. You know the number.'

With a quick wave he went on into the house.

'Look, only one crutch now,' Steve greeted Lizzie with a kiss on the cheek. 'The doctors are very pleased.'

They heard Todd close the door behind him.

'I've been hanging around waiting for you for hours. I think Pearl was starting to get suspicious.' Steve lowered his voice. 'She can be a bit possessive at times.'

'What's all this about?' Lizzie asked.

'It's her birthday next week,' Steve explained, 'and I've arranged for her present to be delivered to Wrenn Cottage. I want it to be a surprise and as there's so much coming and going at the farmhouse I wouldn't be able to find anywhere safe to hide it. Can you take charge of it for me?'

'No problem,' Lizzie assured him.

'I'll try to come and collect it when Pearl's not around. By the way, have you told Todd about our arrangement?'

'No. I don't want word getting round in case Paul Owen finds out where I am so the less people to know the better.'

'I've heard a rumour that Paul's involved with Virginia Winch these days. Did you have a good afternoon out?'

'We went for a walk along the harbour and the time ran away with us.'

'Does this mean what I think it means?' Steve asked with a knowing smile on his face.

'It doesn't mean anything,' Lizzie insisted. 'I'd best be going. Give my love to Pearl.'

'Don't forget, not a word to anyone,' Steve hissed.

'About what?'

'Pearl?' Steve gave a guilty laugh. 'I didn't see you there.'

'Obviously not. What's going on?' she demanded in a voice tight with tears.

'Nothing at all.'

'You promised we wouldn't have secrets from each other. I'm beginning to think Todd's suspicions were correct. He was right about you all along, wasn't he? There is something between the pair of you.'

'You're tired, darling, and it's been a long day.'

'Don't patronise me.' Pearl shook his hand off her elbow.

'Steve,' Lizzie began.

'Leave this to me,' Steve gestured at

her to go. 'Pearl's had words with her father. She's upset. It's nothing I can't handle and thanks for everything.'

Lizzie heard another whimper from Pearl then the front door slamming behind her.

'Just go, Lizzie, please? I'll straighten things out.'

The front door now closed behind Steve leaving Lizzie standing alone in the forecourt. So much for everyone learning to trust each other, she thought as she made her way towards her shiny new van.

Jealousy

'I don't know what's the matter with everyone,' Steve grumbled to Olivia.

'Ease my ankle a bit, darling, there's a good boy.' She was stretched out on her sofa glancing through one of Lizzie's magazines.

'That better?' Steve asked.

'Yes, thank you.' Olivia tossed her magazine to one side. 'Come over here and tell me what's bothering you.'

'Todd's like a bear with a sore head. It's impossible to have a proper conversation with him. He's just snapped at me for no reason and Pearl's not speaking to me either.'

'That's because she suspects you've got a thing going with Lizzie.

'Todd does, too.'

Steve stared at his grandmother in stupefied surprise.

'Don't be ridiculous. I've only just got married.'

'I agree, darling, it does seem a preposterous idea but why else are you having secret assignations with Lizzie?' Olivia enquired.

'I'm not,' he protested.

'You ordered a taxi yesterday afternoon to go to the cottage.'

'Have you been spying on me?' Steve demanded.

'No, but Pearl has and she told me and what's more she told Todd.'

'What exactly did she tell him?'

'That Lizzie is living in your cottage and that you've been visiting her on the quiet.'

'It was only the once.'

'You can't blame your wife, Steve. She's had a tough time convincing that father of hers that you're the perfect husband, then just as he's starting to believe you might be a suitable match for his precious Pearl, she catches you whispering down the telephone in a very furtive manner and cutting off calls the moment she enters the room.'

'What's Todd got to do with any of this? I'm fed up with him interfering in my private life.'

'This is where it gets a bit more complicated,' Olivia explained. 'Really I am very annoyed with you, Steve.'

'Not half as annoyed as I am with Todd. I have not got anything going with Lizzie,' Steve repeated. 'I love Pearl.'

'And Todd loves Lizzie and your thoughtlessness has nearly ruined all my plans.'

'What plans?'

'I had to feign a funny turn on them and almost fall asleep before I could get them to go out to tea. Everything was going fine until you started up all your nonsense with your secret telephone calls and whispered words in private. At times you can be extremely tiresome.'

'For your information, Olivia,' Steve began then stopped speaking.

'What's up?' Olivia demanded as he gaped at her.

'Did you say Todd's in love with Lizzie?'

'I did.'

'That's the second daftest thing I've heard today.'

'Can't you see it in the way he reacts towards her?'

'No, I can't. I never understand anything my brother does.'

'I agree with you there, but take my word for it. He is in love with Lizzie. He may not realise it yet but I'm working on it.'

'You shouldn't go interfering in other people's lives, Olivia.'

'I don't, well, only yours and Todd's and I reckon I'm allowed to do that.'

'That's as may be, but why has Todd got it into his head that I'm entangled with Lizzie?'

'Aren't you listening to a word I've said? It's because you've installed her in your cottage and you've taken to visiting her secretly.'

'I have not.'

'Where were you yesterday afternoon?'

Steve coloured up. 'Well, actually I did meet up with Lizzie.'

'Case proven, I think.'

'It's not what you think it is.'

'It's not me you've got to convince. It's Todd.'

'Lizzie didn't want anyone to know where she was because of this Paul Owen man who won't stop following her around, but Pearl knew all about it, not about Paul, but she agreed that Lizzie could occupy the cottage until we are ready to move in.'

'Did Todd know of this arrangement?'

'No, but only because Lizzie didn't want him to. You weren't supposed to know either.'

'There's nothing that goes on in this house that I don't know about.'

'You can say that again,' Steve muttered.

'You'd better go and put things right with your brother.'

'I don't see why I should and I've nothing to make up.' Steve looked like a small boy in trouble at school.

'Yes you have.'

'Todd started it. Do you know he said I didn't have the brains I was born with? All because I made an innocent comment about him getting a girlfriend then Pearl and I could make up a foursome and we could all go out for the evening.'

'If you don't make things up with your brother, I'll knock your heads together.'

'It'll blow over. It always has before,' Steve said, determined to hold his ground.

'Am I not getting through to you?'

'Perhaps you are,' Steve admitted, scratching the side of his plaster. 'I can't wait to the get this thing off. It's driving me mad, only another week to go, thank goodness. Then perhaps things can get back to normal. So,' he mused, 'Todd and Lizzie. In a way it makes sense.

They're both very independent. You know you could be right, Olivia.'

'I'm always right,' Olivia replied. 'And what are we going to do now?'

'About what?'

'Todd and Lizzie.'

'Did someone mention my name?'

Steve whirled round at the sound of his brother's voice behind him. 'Olivia's been telling me you think I'm having an affair with Lizzie.'

'It's none of my business what you get up to with Lizzie, but you ought to have a word with Pearl and put her right if it's not true,' Todd replied calmly.

'Of course it's not true. What do you take me for, or Lizzie come to that?'

'I'm merely wondering what Lizzie is doing holed up in Wrenn Close and why no-one told me of your arrangement.'

'Because this is exactly the sort of reaction she suspected she would get from you after that business with the newspaper interview, and for your information, Pearl knew where Lizzie was all along. She agreed to the plan. I was totally up front about it from the start.'

The connecting door to Steve and Pearl's flat opened and a blonde whirlwind in a pink dress flew into the room.

Steve hobbled to his feet. 'What on earth are you wearing?'

'I thought you'd forgotten. It's my birthday present, isn't it?'

Pearl threw her arms around Steve's neck. He toppled backwards and landed back in the soft chair he had recently vacated, with Pearl on top of him.

'You're suffocating me,' he protested.

'Sorry.' Pearl danced to her feet. 'Don't you think it's the most beautiful dress in the world? Olivia?'

She did a twirl for the older woman's benefit.

'You look lovely, dear,' Olivia said in a soft voice, 'but then you would look stunning wearing a sack.'

'Steve and I were window shopping and we saw it on display in an exclusive boutique.'

'I went back for it,' Steve explained, 'while you were on the telephone to your father. They had to order it in especially from Paris, as it's a model and it was supposed to be a present for your birthday which isn't until tomorrow,' he pointed out.

'I found it in the back of your wardrobe.'

'What were you doing there?'

Pearl had the grace to blush as she explained, 'I was looking in your pockets for evidence.'

'Of what?'

'You know credit card slips, lipstick stains on a shirt?'

Olivia made a noise of disbelief. 'You've been watching too many trashy films, my girl, and I'll have you know my grandson would never behave in such a cavalier manner.'

'I'm sorry I've been so horrible to you, Steve. I should have trusted you.'

'Yes, you should, but for your and Todd's benefit, let me explain. A dress box isn't the easiest thing in the world to hide, so I arranged for it to be delivered to the cottage. Lizzie promised to take it in for me and keep it until I went to collect it. I thought it would be safe for one day in the back of my wardrobe.' He pulled a face. 'Obviously I was wrong and so were you, Todd.' He glared at his brother. 'So there you have it.'

'Thank goodness we're all friends again,' Olivia said with a smile.

The clock on the mantelpiece chimed the hour. 'Heavens, I'm late.' Pearl leapt up.

'Now where are you off to?' Steve asked.

'I promised I'd look in on my father. He's got a present for me, too. You don't mind, do you?'

'Anything to keep him sweet,' Steve replied.

'I'll put my dress back in the box.' Pearl was all smiles. 'You can give it to me properly tomorrow. By the way, talking of Lizzie I bumped into a friend of hers earlier. He was hanging around the gate.'

'What friend?' Todd asked in an anxious voice.

'Paul somebody or other. I didn't catch the surname. He said he wanted a word with Lizzie. I told him he would probably find her in the cottage working on Jessie's curtains. He knew all about the party so I didn't see the harm in telling him she had moved. Anyway, must dash. See you later.' She blew Steve a kiss before disappearing in a waft of French perfume.

'She means Paul Owen,' Steve said.

'I know that,' Todd snapped back at him.

'Hadn't you better do something about it then?' Steve retaliated, 'instead of sitting around here accusing me of having an affair with Lizzie?'

'It's not my place to interfere.'

'The man's fixated on her. That's why she was working late in the unit in the first place and why she didn't want anyone to know where she'd gone after she moved out of her flat. You have a responsibility towards her.'

'Steve's right,' Olivia cut in. 'Somebody ought to check up on her.'

'I can't drive with this leg. It's got to be you.'

'I agree it's probably a fuss about nothing,' Olivia said, 'but to put my mind at rest? Todd? Please?' she coaxed. 'If you need an excuse for calling say I want to reschedule our tea date and I've lost her mobile number.'

★　★　★

Lizzie stretched her aching back. At last Jessie's curtains were now completed to her revised requirements. More than ever pleased that she had structured generous terms of payment for the commission, she rubbed the back of her neck. Crouching over a sewing machine for hours on end was not good for her posture.

Steve's work was next on her list, after which she promised herself a holiday. It had been ages since she had got together with Florence and her mother. She would email them both tonight to see if they could arrange anything.

She spooned instant coffee into a mug, annoyed that she couldn't shake off a pang of disappointment that there had been no word from Todd since their cable car trip. Pride had prevented her from asking Steve how he was.

Why she should expect Todd to seek her out she didn't know. He was the most challenging, infuriating and controlling man she had ever met. Paul had been the same with his younger brother Mark. Lizzie poured boiling water into her cup. Except Paul's intentions had been tainted with malice.

Lizzie swept recalcitrant locks of hair away from her face. Along with everything else a trip to her stylist was long overdue. Strolling back into the lounge she picked up her mobile. A flash of sunlight on a car windscreen caught her attention as it drew up outside. Her fingers froze halfway through dialling Jessie's number.

Paul Owen was getting out the car. He smiled as he saw her looking out of the window and waved a greeting before crossing the pavement and heading towards her front door.

Apologies

'Hello, Lizzie,' Paul greeted her. 'I've brought you a peace offering.'

He thrust a bunch of dahlias at her. Damp petals tickled her face.

'They are your favourites, aren't they? Red gold, like your hair?'

Lizzie had never seen Paul look so unsure of himself. His blue eyes didn't look in the least bit menacing as an anxious smile hovered on his lips.

'How did you find me?' Lizzie demanded.

'I bumped into that new wife of Steve's at Maiden Farm.'

'Pearl?'

'I happened to mention that I was looking for you and,' he spread his arms, 'here I am. I've been looking for you everywhere but it was as if you'd disappeared off the face of the earth. I didn't know what to do. I thought I'd never see you again. I know that's what you wanted but, look, do you think I could come inside and explain?'

Lizzie blinked at him. She had seen Paul in many moods but nothing to match this.

'Is there any particular reason why I should?' she asked, reluctant to trust him.

'I don't want to say what I've got to say standing on your doorstep. Virginia knows I'm here,' he added as if hoping her name would lend weight to his request. 'She helped me choose the flowers.'

The expensive cellophane crackled as Lizzie clutched the bouquet to her chest. She twined a curly piece of golden ribbon around her fingers. This was no petrol filling station bunch of flowers. She spotted a small box of Belgian chocolates nestling inside the wrapping.

'I was about to make some coffee.' Lizzie hoped Paul would turn down her offer.

'Then may I join you?' he asked, an eager look on his face. 'What I've got to say won't take long.'

Reluctantly Lizzie opened the door wide and Paul followed her down the hall.

'This is Steve Baxter's new cottage — right?'

Lizzie placed the flowers in a bowl then poured some water over the base of the stalks to keep them fresh before stirring coffee into a mug. Paul perched on a stool.

'I'm sorting out the colour scheme for him before he and Pearl move in.'

'Good idea,' Paul enthused. 'It's a nice property. Virginia and I want to look for something similar.'

Lizzie sat on the other stool opposite Paul and looked expectantly at him.

'I don't know where to start,' he admitted, then cleared his throat. 'Would you believe I'm actually here to apologise?'

'That would take some believing,' Lizzie agreed.

'I sort of started to at Maiden Farm

but things spiralled out of control, didn't they?' He gave an embarrassed laugh. 'Next thing I knew we had a situation on our hands. I know what happened was largely my fault.'

'It was completely your fault.' Lizzie saw no reason to let Paul off the hook.

'You can't make me feel any worse than I do. You don't have to remind me that our last meeting was a little undignified.'

'Paul, where is this all leading?'

'I'm getting there.'

Lizzie's mobile buzzed signalling an incoming call.

'Leave it,' Paul ordered as she went to pick it up.

'It may be important.'

'So is this.'

The blue eyes flashed reminding Lizzie that for all his fine words Paul had a short fuse and didn't like his plans thwarted.

'I won't be much longer, I promise,' he softened the tone of his voice.

Lizzie sat down again and waited for

him to continue.

'When I learned you'd had to leave your flat as well as your work unit my conscience went into overdrive. I thought first of all you were being evicted because of me.'

'Why?' Lizzie frowned.

'Because I'd hung around outside. I didn't make a nuisance of myself but I saw that young girl, Charlie I think she was called, anyway I saw her tweaking the curtains one night and I knew I'd been spotted.'

'My move was actually nothing to do with you.'

'I realise that now, but the situation made me feel a bit grubby. Anyway by way of making amends I telephoned the local newspaper to ask if they could print a retraction about that interview but they said it didn't form part of their current policy.'

Paul sat back expectantly.

'Paul, I appreciate the gesture and the flowers are lovely. Now I have things to do.'

'I talked things over with Virginia. She said I should clear things up between us before we moved our relationship forward. I think it was her way of making sure you and I had no baggage. There isn't any, is there?' he faltered.

'I'm willing to put the past behind us if you are.'

He broke into a relieved smile. 'I know I don't deserve such generosity but if there's anything I can do for you, you only have to let me know.'

Lizzie did her best not to raise her eyebrows in surprise.

'Thank you and give my regards to Virginia.' She stood up, unable to think of anything else to say.

'Perhaps we could all meet up some time?' Paul suggested.

'My plans are a bit up in the air at the moment.'

'Right, of course, well I'd best be going.' Lizzie breathed a silent sigh of relief as Paul finally took the hint. 'You know,' he paused, 'when Mark and I were young our parents were busy building up the business and it fell to me to look after my younger brother. The same way, I suppose, Todd took it on himself to look after Steve. It's difficult to let go of the reins once everyone starts growing up. When Mark introduced you and I after I'd broken up with a girlfriend I was jealous. It's not something I'm proud of, but I did put obstacles in the way of your relationship with my brother.'

'You did a thorough job,' Lizzie admitted.

'I'm not trying to make myself feel better about what I did or sound disloyal to my brother,' Paul said, 'but Mark isn't a leader. He's happy to do as our parents ask and he always falls in with their plans. That's why he's a success in the family business. He does as he's told, you don't.'

Similar thoughts had crossed Lizzie's mind in the past but there seemed little point in voicing them now.

'Anyway,' Paul continued, 'I'm going

to have to buckle down from now on. Virginia,' he seemed to be searching for the right words, 'thinks it would be a good idea,' he finished with a shame-faced smile. 'By the way, I have told my parents that the things printed about you were,' he paused, 'misinterpreted.'

'Thank you,' Lizzie replied.

'Goodbye then.'

Paul brushed his lips against her cheek then appeared to lose his balance. He stumbled against her.

'Paul, what's wrong?' Lizzie asked in concern.

It was then she saw an arm locked around his chest.

'Let me go.' Paul struggled against his assailant. 'What are you playing at?'

'Todd,' Lizzie called out, recognising his wristwatch, 'let him go.'

Without warning Paul fell forward into Lizzie's arms. She could hear Todd breathing heavily behind him.

'Pearl told him where you were.' He gulped. 'Olivia got in a panic. You didn't answer your mobile. I thought he might be,' he gulped again, 'causing more trouble.'

Paul managed to straighten his collar then smoothed down his ruffled hair.

'What do you think you're playing at, Baxter?' he demanded.

'Are you all right?' Lizzie asked in concern as his colour returned to normal.

'Fine, no thanks to you.' He glared at Todd. 'What's your problem?'

'I thought you were annoying Miss Hilton.'

'For your information I was saying goodbye to her.'

'You were kissing her.'

'On the cheek, and what business is it of yours?'

'You've been hanging around her far too much.'

'And I'm now going before one of us says or does something they regret. Keep in touch.' He nodded at Lizzie then scuttled off towards his car.

'What is going on?' Lizzie demanded.

'I thought,' Todd jutted out his jaw,

the uncomfortable look on his face deepening, 'I don't know what I thought, but when I saw him standing on your doorstep kissing you I knew I had to stop him.'

Lizzie let out a sigh. 'You'd better come in. Goodness knows what the neighbours will think of all this.'

For the second time that afternoon, Lizzie's footsteps echoed down the bare corridor as she headed towards the kitchen. She threw two mugs of cold coffee down the sink then reheated some water.

'How did you find out where I was?' she asked, her head still buzzing.

Todd shuffled from foot to foot in the confines of Steve's small kitchen.

'Steve told me.'

'He promised not to reveal my whereabouts.'

'He had to because Pearl found her dress. In the back of the wardrobe,' Todd added, looking expectantly at Lizzie as if that explained everything.

'Todd, sit down.'

Todd did as he was told.

'Steve hid it there,' he continued mulishly as if he wanted to get the explanation off his chest. 'It's her birthday tomorrow. It was the dress that started it all. She was looking for evidence.'

There was none of the smooth businessman about Todd now. He looked as thoroughly confused as Lizzie felt.

'Evidence of what?' Lizzie nudged a fresh mug of hot coffee towards Todd.

'Pearl overheard Steve talking furtively on the telephone. He hung up when she walked into the room and wouldn't tell her what it was all about. So she checked the last number called. It was here.' Todd tried to sip his coffee but it was too hot. He banged the mug back down on the table. 'You do understand, don't you?'

'There's no need to go on.' Lizzie stalled Todd from embarking on further confusing explanations. 'There are a few gaps, but I'm getting the picture.'

Todd picked up his coffee then put it down again still without drinking a drop.

'When Pearl told us Paul had been down at the gate asking after you, Olivia got worried. She thought he was up to his old tricks. Steve still can't drive and Pearl had a date with her father. That only left me.'

'To come galloping to my rescue?'

'I know you don't need it,' Todd protested, 'but Steve was making noises about driving over. Then that would have started Pearl off again.' Todd picked up his mug for the third time and mumbled, 'Besides I wanted to see you.'

'Put that wretched coffee down before you spill the lot,' Lizzie ordered him as she mopped up the liquid seeping into table then jumped as Todd put out a hand and trapped her fingers under his.

Lizzie's heart thumped painfully in her chest as she forgot to breathe.

'What are you doing?'

'Lizzie, I don't know where to start.'

Lizzie tried to get her hand back but Todd wouldn't let go.

'I know what it's like having to fend for yourself, and everybody else,' he added.

His brown eyes were fixed on her in an unwavering stare as if willing Lizzie to understand.

'That's why I think you're the most wonderful girl I've ever met.'

'What?' Lizzie jolted upright but Todd didn't give her the chance to say any more.

'You've coped with a potential stalker, personal damage to your character, a broken engagement, a demanding job, being homeless.'

'I'm not homeless,' Lizzie protested.

'And on top of that you've had me casting aspersions on your character. Most people would have given up. I know,' Todd stalled her interruption, 'you don't do giving up.'

'Well, thank you for the character analysis.' Lizzie finally managed to get a word in edgewise.

'I suppose, because I've been responsible for my family for so long, I found it difficult to change my ways.'

'I haven't asked you to,' Lizzie pointed out.

'I mean, there's Olivia, she's one of the best and Monty could keep an eye on her while he was alive but without him she reverted to her old ways. She's extravagant, warm-hearted and an absolute sucker for a hard luck story.'

It was as well Todd carried on speaking as his words temporarily robbed Lizzie of the power of speech.

'If she suspects I'm trying to keep an eye on her she can get sneaky. What with her and Steve to look after,' Todd picked up a teaspoon then put it back on the table, 'it's not easy and it hasn't left me with much time for personal relationships of my own.'

'Is that why you were so distrustful of me when we first met?' Lizzie felt a pang of pity for Todd. She could imagine how she would have behaved had she been placed in the same situation with her mother and sister. They were three very different characters, too.

'In the past Steve has been as gullible as Olivia. You've seen what he's like, running off to get married without telling anyone. I was tired and in your case my judgement was flawed,' he admitted.

Lizzie stopped Todd from launching into another explanation of his family's failings by putting a hand up to touch his face.

'I'm glad Steve and Pearl are reconciled and I'm sorry if I played any part in causing trouble between them. When he asked me to accept his parcel I had no idea of the trouble it would cause.'

'Hang the wretched parcel.' Todd made a gesture with his hand and more coffee slopped on to the tabletop.

Lizzie deftly removed the mug from his reach.

'I wanted to throttle Paul when I saw

him kissing you.'

'You very nearly succeeded, and for your information it was Virginia Winch's idea that he should wipe the slate clean by apologising to me. He wants to move on from the past and so do I.'

'Would you consider,' Todd struggled with his words, 'moving back to Maiden Farm? No strings attached?'

Throughout their exchange Lizzie's mobile phone had been constantly signalling incoming messages.

'I really do have to answer that call,' she apologised.

'No.'

'Yes.' Lizzie wrestled her hand out of Todd's hold.

'Darling,' Jessie sounded relieved. 'Thank goodness. I was beginning to think you weren't ever going to talk to me again after our little difference of opinion.'

Todd crossed his arms and glared at Lizzie from across the kitchen table.

'You've done my curtains, I hope? Good. I'm in such a tizz. My niece has arrived from America. Stephanie, you remember my mentioning her? She wants to get in touch with Todd. Olivia said he's with you. He absolutely must come to the party. I think Stephanie's still in love with him, you know. Can you put him on the line?'

'It's Jessie for you.' Lizzie handed over her mobile. 'She's got Stephanie on the line. Apparently she's still in love with you.'

Crossed Wires

Lizzie's face ached from smiling at so many of Jessie's guests. Their hostess hadn't stinted on hospitality and everyone was well refreshed after a rousing chorus of *Happy Birthday* to Danny who lapped up all the attention.

True to her word Jessie had promoted Lizzie's work and there were no more business cards left in her clutch bag. She felt tired and wondered how soon it would be before she could take a respectable leave of the proceedings. She wasn't used to parties and this one was giving her a headache.

In the distance she caught sight of Paul with Virginia Winch clinging onto his arm. The marquee had been a big success as the day was overcast and although the forecasted showers hadn't materialised there had been several spots of rain during the late afternoon, enough to send guests scurrying for cover.

'There you are.'

Lizzie didn't immediately turn round at the sound of a female voice behind her. The drawing room was a seething mass of guests, all of whom seemed to prefer it to the marquee now the wind was getting up and buffeting the tent flaps.

'I am right, aren't I? You are Lizzie Hilton?'

A warm hand was placed on her arm as she was attempting to discreetly push back her sleeve to check the time on her watch.

'I'm Stephanie Cox, Stephanie Winter that was. I would introduce you to my husband, but I appear to have lost him. How are you getting on with the Baxters? Mad bunch, aren't they?'

Stephanie was wearing enormous framed glasses and beaming at Lizzie with a huge open smile.

'You've seen Todd?' Lizzie asked carefully.

'I have indeed. The one that got away.'

'You were engaged to him, I believe?' Lizzie didn't quite know why the knowledge that Stephanie was still in love with Todd should hurt so much.

'Want to know a secret?' Stephanie leaned forward and lowered her voice. 'It was actually Steve I fancied, but I guess I'm not his sort. I'm plump and I wear glasses. I've lost a bit of weight since those days.' Stephanie smoothed down her elegant dress. 'I have my hair styled now by a qualified hairdresser, but underneath it all I'm still the plain Jane I always was and Steve doesn't go for that sort of girl.

'To save face I pretended it was Todd I fancied, but we both knew it wasn't going to happen. He was very kind to me and took me out and about and introduced me to people, then Hal appeared on the scene and, wow, I certainly knew what love was about. I think that's why I lost weight. I couldn't eat, couldn't sleep. I really got it bad. I don't suppose for one moment I broke Todd's heart. The story got about that I was interested in Hal's oil wells. I mean, really,' She gave a loud laugh that had heads turning their way. 'He has got one, but it's so small you need sat nav to find it. We're certainly not up there with the big boys, but that was Todd's face saver and I felt I owed him, so I let the story stand and there you have it. The history of our affair such as it was.'

'I, well, thank you for telling me all this.'

'I heard Jessie saying I was still in love with Todd. Sorry about that. Everything Jessie does is over the top. Have you seen poor old Danny trying to cope with talking to people he hasn't seen for years? Jessie has pushed the boat out. By the way I love your curtains. I've got one of your little cards so if ever you're thinking of going global let me know and I'll put the word round Texas for you.' Stephanie glanced over her shoulder. 'I'd better go find Hal. He's more used to roping steer than attending social occasions. Bye.'

Lizzie watched Stephanie disappear into the crowd, her heart racing. Were she and Todd destined to keep going round in circles because they were both so independent?

Lizzie had insisted on making her own way to Jessie's party after she heard Stephanie issue a telephone invitation to Todd.

'I wouldn't want to spoil your reunion,' she'd said by way of explanation, 'and I need to drive myself over to the party in my own van.'

'Next thing you'll be telling me,' Todd had muttered, 'is that you're using the tradesmen's entrance.'

'That's me, trade.'

It had been a mean retort and left Lizzie feeling cheap. After Jessie's telephone call Lizzie had cleared away the coffee mugs and Todd had driven back to Maiden Farm, not bothering to wave at her before he clambered into his car.

She tried to spot Todd amongst the crowd of people milling around the lawn. Her behaviour had been immature and she owed him an apology.

Understanding Each Other

Thunder rumbled around the hills and the sky darkened reducing visibility. Several people cast anxious glances upwards as lightning split the distant sky. Another crack of thunder followed by vicious spikes of rain hit the terrace starting a human stampede towards the house. From the marquee came the sound of crashing china.

Pandemonium followed as guests struggled to find cover.

'What's happened?' Lizzie grabbed at a guest's elbow.

'I think a table's collapsed,' Virginia Winch shrieked, rushing in from the garden, her hair plastered to her head. 'Where's Paul? Have you seen him?'

'He was on the lawn a few moments ago,' Lizzie replied.

The two girls fought their way through the oncoming guests and into the marquee. The scene that met their eyes was one of absolute confusion.

Floral decorations had been ground underfoot in muddy puddles and two dogs were busily gorging the crumbled mess of icing sugar, dried fruit and marzipan that had been Danny's birthday cake.

The wind whistled around the struts and the chandeliers swayed, creating ghostly patterns on the frightened faces of the staff who were doing their best to save the situation. One of the serving tables had buckled under the weight of the buffet and now lay in a heap surrounded by broken glass, bottles and the remains of the cold spread.

'Get everyone into the house,' Paul ordered a frightened looking Virginia, 'now,' he barked when she didn't immediately move.

The waiters didn't need to be told twice and the few remaining guests scuttled out of the tent.

'What are you going to do?' Lizzie demanded.

'Make sure the struts are safe. They should hold and I hope it's only a passing storm, but we don't want any more accidents.'

'Want any help?' Todd shouted over as he chased the dogs out of the marquee. 'What a mess.' He looked down at the remains of Danny's cake on the grass.

'Good man, another pair of hands is always welcome.' Paul ducked as one of the crystals parted company from the chandelier and fell on to the grass. 'Can you get the lights down? They're looking dangerous. I'll be outside if you need me.'

'Go and get a ladder.' Todd pushed Lizzie towards the tent flaps.

'There isn't time,' Lizzie protested. 'If you stand on a chair I'll hold on to your legs.'

'Don't be silly, you'll do yourself an injury.'

'Stop arguing and get up there,' Lizzie insisted, unfolding a chair. 'This should hold your weight.'

The storm was now overhead and a vicious crack of thunder made the ground vibrate under their feet.

Todd scrambled onto the wooden chair and perching on the slats began undoing the fittings that held the light in place. Lizzie could feel the muscles in his legs straining as she held on.

'Done it. Can you help take the weight while I get down?'

Outside the sound of shouting voices grew louder as several of the male guests ran to help Paul reinforce the struts.

The storm ripped a slash in the canvas and rain poured through the gaping hole.

'Get back inside the house,' Todd ordered as he dragged the chandelier to one side.

'We've got to get the second one down,' Lizzie insisted as the remaining light flickered, faded then went out. Without the hum of the generator in the background, the world went very quiet. Todd and Lizzie stared at each other in the semi darkness. Both were breathing heavily.

'There's a cut on your forehead.' She put out a hand to touch Todd's wound. 'You're bleeding.'

'And you look like a drowned seal.' He paused. 'You're not going to do as I say and go inside with the other guests, are you?' he asked, a resigned note to his voice.

'Not while you're still out here risking life and limb for a chandelier.'

'Come on then, but steady. The ground is seriously slippery now. I don't know if this chair will stand my weight much longer.'

The legs sank into the mud as Todd climbed up again.

'Can't see what I'm doing.' His voice was a deep growl. 'The fixture's knotted up.'

The light creaked as it swayed above them.

'Please, Todd,' she begged, her heart in her mouth, 'take care.'

'It matters to you, does it, what

happens to me?'

His legs jerked against hers as he strained to undo the fixture.

'Of course it does,' Lizzie replied. Todd stopped struggling. 'I wouldn't want anything to happen to you. I love you.'

Her words were drowned in a sea of water as the top of the marquee gave way under the weight of the storm. Todd undid the final light mooring. It crashed on to the grass. The chair collapsed under him.

Todd fell into Lizzie's arms. The weight of his body sent her toppling backwards on to the muddy grass.

'I suppose you wouldn't mind repeating that?' Todd's breath was warm against her face as Lizzie attempted to untangle her limbs from his, 'I didn't catch all you said.'

Lizzie tried to struggle against his weight but he pinioned her body to the ground with his.

'Can't you move? Are you all right?' She gulped, trying to breathe normally.

'Never felt better,' Todd replied as his lips descended on hers.

The thud of his heartbeat was as relentless as a drill against the flimsy material of her blouse.

'I, er, hate to interrupt.' The sound of someone clearing their throat drew them apart. Paul was smiling at them from a gap in the canvas. 'Health and safety think it might be a good idea if we abandoned ship, so if you've nothing better to do may I suggest you take their advice?'

'Be with you in a minute,' Todd replied, his eyes never leaving Lizzie's face.

'Don't leave it too long,' Paul advised. 'If the marquee should blow away, you could find yourselves the focus of about fifty pairs of interested eyes.'

'Stop wriggling,' Todd instructed Lizzie.

'We've got to do as he says,' she insisted.

'Why?'

'It's cold and wet and I'm lying on something unpleasant.'

'Did you mean what you said when I was performing acrobatics on that wretched chair?' Lizzie stopped moving. Todd's image swam before her eyes. She blinked moisture from her lashes. 'Forgotten? Then let me refresh your memory. You said you loved me. Do you?'

'Yes,' the word tumbled from her lips.

An infuriatingly complacent smile crossed Todd's face.

'Goodness knows why,' she added. 'You're the most infuriating, self controlling, suspicious person I have ever met in my life.'

'I totally agree with you,' Todd replied, his stubble scratching Lizzie's cheek, 'and it takes one to know one.'

'What do you mean?'

'You are the most independent, spiky, organisational, beautiful woman I have ever met in my life and I have to admit I'm mad about you, too, and if this blasted marquee hadn't thrown a hissy fit I was going to come and find you and tell you.'

'Do you think,' Lizzie gulped, 'we could discuss our feelings in more comfortable surroundings?'

'Come on then.' Todd eased his weight off Lizzie and dragged her to her feet. 'Although I have to warn you this might be the last time I do anything you tell me.'

'I wouldn't be too sure about that.' Lizzie shivered.

Todd put his arm around her shoulders. The warmth from his body seeped into hers.

'You look like a spaniel when your hair's wet,' he teased.

'I wouldn't like to say what you look like. You're dripping from head to foot.' Lizzie nuzzled in closer.

'Anything else you want to get off your chest?' Todd asked.

'There is one thing.'

'If it's to do with contracts can we reschedule to a later date?'

'It's to do with your inheritance.'

'Not that old chestnut again.'

'When we get married,' Lizzie began.

'I don't believe I asked you,' Todd replied.

'Will you marry me?' Lizzie asked.

'I knew it,' Todd crowed, 'You were after the inheritance all along, weren't you?'

'I want you to use the money to set up a trust fund to make provision for people starting out in business.'

'If I do that you realise we won't be able to afford a place of our own and we'll have to live with Olivia probably for ever?'

'That's exactly what I had in mind,' Lizzie said with a happy sigh.

'In that case,' Todd replied, kissing her again, 'I accept your proposal.'

THE END

We do hope that you have enjoyed reading this large print book.

Did you know that all of our titles are available for purchase?

We publish a wide range of high quality large print books including:
Romances, Mysteries, Classics
General Fiction
Non Fiction and Westerns

Special interest titles available in large print are:
The Little Oxford Dictionary
Music Book, Song Book
Hymn Book, Service Book

Also available from us courtesy of Oxford University Press:
Young Readers' Dictionary
(large print edition)
Young Readers' Thesaurus
(large print edition)

For further information or a free brochure, please contact us at:
Ulverscroft Large Print Books Ltd.,
The Green, Bradgate Road, Anstey,
Leicester, LE7 7FU, England.
Tel: (00 44) 0116 236 4325
Fax: (00 44) 0116 234 0205

BRIEF ECSTASY

Denise Robins

Rosemary takes a job in Spain, as a companion to Mercedes. Then, on the brief few hours train journey to Malaga, Rosemary meets Paul and falls completely under his spell. But her dreams of love are shattered when she meets Mercedes, and learns of her engagement to Paul. Hurt and angry, Rosemary hatches a devious plan. Heavily veiled, she changes places with the bride at Mercedes' wedding to Paul — but the consequences are quite different to how she had imagined . . .

THE TURNING POINT

Phyllis Mallett

Barbara Taylor is on holiday, incognito, at the hotel her company has recently failed to take over. There she meets Jim Farrell, the harassed owner, and his young daughter Leanne. Then, fate intervenes in their lives and undercurrents threaten them. Barbara becomes so involved with the family that telling the truth about herself could shatter her new-found happiness — but eventually, when all is revealed, she can only hope that love will be kind to her.